At Night He Remembers

ALSO BY JAMES CUNNEEN

Seven Principles of Ministry for the Average Radical Christian
(Wipf and Stock, 2011)

20 Questions About Ministry
(Wipf and Stock, 2018)

At Night He Remembers

JAMES CUNNEEN

RESOURCE *Publications* · Eugene, Oregon

AT NIGHT HE REMEMBERS

Resource Publications
An Imprint of Wipf and Stock Publishers
199 W. 8th Ave., Suite 3
Eugene, OR 97401

www.wipfandstock.com

PAPERBACK ISBN: 978-1-6667-7878-6
HARDCOVER ISBN: 978-1-6667-7879-3
EBOOK ISBN: 978-1-6667-7880-9

VERSION NUMBER 060723

Unless otherwise noted, "Scripture references, including paraphrases, are taken from the New American Standard Bible © 1960, 1963 1968, 1971, 1973, 1975, 1977 by The Lockman Foundation. Used by permission" (www.lockman.org)

The poem quoted in Part 4, "The Honesty of Winter" is taken from *Winter Nights, Falling,* by John Hazard, Naming A Stranger, Kelsay Books, Aldrich Press, 2015

Used by permission.

The locations and some events in this book are part of the author's experiences. All characters and situations are ficticious. Questions or comments? Email the author at LTLcunneen@gmail.com

To all who serve the Lord

Prologue

Sister Angelique crossed the coast road and made her way to a damaged concrete bench on the beach. She sat almost motionless for several minutes before beginning the simple lunch she'd brought with her. Even in this time of war, the beach at Nha Trang was beautiful. As a girl in France, she had loved going to the beach with her father and brothers. And here, watching the gentle waves of the South China Sea, she felt strangely at peace.

As she did each day, she watched for activity at the Hotel Grand, now a headquarters of the American Army. A jeep and driver pulled up to the front entrance of the hotel, and an American soldier got in. The jeep drove away.

Sister Angelique prayed in French for the soldier. "Holy Father, and Mary, Mother of God, You know who that is. Please let him live and please don't let him kill anyone. Permit him please to be a person for You." Sister prayed this prayer for three soldiers she saw that afternoon, as she did most days. Then she rose and began walking slowly up the coast road to the convent school where she taught. She had been in Viet Nam for 13 years and had prayed for hundreds of soldiers. The first soldier she prayed for on this day was Lieutenant Jacob Saith.

The Firebase

Central Highlands, Viet Nam, 1969

"I DON'T like this place."

Warrant Officer Gibbs, piloting the Huey, was nervous. They'd gotten a late start, and the tiny firebase had a bad approach at the best of times. Now, with shadows covering the foliage that fell off to the East, the chances of getting shot at were greater, though still unlikely.

"Why?"

" It's the East slope. The tree line is so close to the LZ."

" I see what you mean," said his passenger. First Lieutenant Jacob Saith glanced at WO Gibbs. 'Unbelievable,' Jacob thought, 'he's *so* young. Maybe 20. Flying a Huey!' Then he paid attention to their approach to LZ Polly; it might be the only time in the next five months he'd get to see the whole terrain from the air.

"Lieutenant, if you don't mind getting off fast, I want to get back to Pleiku before dark."

Jacob nodded. "You got it. Thanks for the ride."

They swung around to avoid the east slope, and touched down with the usual storm of dust. WO Gibbs wasn't kidding when he said he wanted to leave quickly. He was spinning up the rotors while Jacob was twisting his lanky, six-foot frame around to grab his duffel bag from the back. Jacob jumped out, dragging the duffel, and the Huey was off low, cranking into a hard left turn. It was a bigger target down low, but a much faster one.

Jacob slung his duffel bag over his shoulder and made his way through the day-time gap in the perimeter wire to where a sergeant stood waiting for him.

'What?' Jacob thought, 'a first sergeant . . . on this little base.' The first sergeant was medium height, solid, with a hard-as-nails expression.

Aloud, Jacob said, "First Sergeant, how are you? I'm your new FDO."

First Sergeant LaFleur saluted. "Welcome to LZ Polly, Lieutenant. But no, sir, you're not."

"Not what?"

"The new Fire Direction Officer. You're the new Commanding Officer, Lieutenant. Well, actually, you're the new Executive Officer of Charlie Battery. But you're the CO of this place. We just got the twix from Pleiku. Captain Guidry got stuck in Saigon coming back from R&R, and they figured he's too short to send back to the field."

'Good grief, Jacob thought, trying to quickly get used to the idea of being in command of the firebase. He noticed the first sergeant watching him closely. "Thanks, First Sergeant, I'm glad to be here."

The first sergeant seemed to relax.

Jacob looked at the guns on the tiny base. Only three. And . . . oh, man, he realized, they're not 105's!

"First Sergeant, are those 155's?"

The first sergeant nodded. "Yes, sir! Fresh from Rock Island Arsenal, vintage 1941." Then he added, seriously, "But these old howitzers are good, really good."

"Okay, First Sergeant. But I haven't laid a battery since Fort Sill. And I know nothing about 155's. I'd sure appreciate your help on that."

" Yes, sir! Oh, and I know you've been in the field, so you know this, but with your permission, that'll be my last salute for a while"

Jabob laughed. "Of course, First Sergeant. Do we have an FDO?"

"Lt. Tillinghast came out yesterday. He's the new Fire Direction Officer."

"Lt. Tillinghast?"

"Yes, sir. Do you know him?"

"Well, if it's the same one," Jacob said. "I knew him in OCS."

Jacob thought. 'Tillinghast! It's gotta be him with that name.' In Officer Candidate School, upperclassman Tillinghast was one of those who seemed to delight in tormenting lowerclassmen, among whom had been OC Jacob Saith.

First Sergeant said, heading for the mess tent. "Let me give you the tour. You'll be with me in the CO bunker."

Landing Zone Polly, nicknamed, of course, LZ Potty, was a remote firebase with only three howitzers, half of Charlie Battery, the rest of which was in Pleiku. LZ Polly was probably less than two acres, encircled by two rows of razor wire. From the air, it looked like a scab on the green rolling land. There were two pull-apart 'gates' in the wire, one for the path to a nearby village, and one at the helicopter landing site, just outside the perimeter wire. The village gate was open during the day to let the village women come and go with the washing. A good portion of the perimeter wire on the village side usually looked like a clothesline. It was where the women hung the soldiers' fatigues to dry.

In theory, the firebase was accessible by road, from the village to Pleiku, but no supplies ever came that way. It was too dangerous. All supplies came by helicopter, including the huge sling loads of gas and artillery shells, brought by Chinooks. Mail and food came by Hueys, known as 'slicks.'

First Sergeant LaFleur introduced him to the three gun crews. No one jumped to attention or saluted. This was an isolated base and some military formalities were dispensed with. The sole concern of the NCO's and officers was efficiency. Jacob knew he'd get to know more about the strengths and weaknesses of the crews from the first sergeant later on. The gun captains were sergeants and the men were mostly PFC's and corporals. There was even an assigned medic, Specialist Yoder, which was rare for such a small firebase.

The guns on LZ Polly were vintage WWII 155mm howitzers. They were the largest caliber artillery piece that could be moved by helicopter—the big Skycranes—so a normal six-howitzer battery was often split up and little LZ's sprang up all over the Central Highlands.

There were four bunkers on the LZ. The two largest were living quarters for the men; next in size was the FDC, the Fire Direction Center; the smallest was the CO bunker, where First Sergeant LaFleur, and now Jacob, lived. All were simply holes dug in the ground by Army engineer bulldozers, sided and covered over by massive steel plating, and a couple of feet of dirt. They easily withstood mortar rounds, and were quite comfortable. Everyone slept under mosquito netting, not so much for mosquitos—which were not a big problem in the Central Highlands—but because of rats. There were a lot of rats.

In the following weeks, Jacob quickly adjusted to the unfamiliar position of being in charge of the tiny base. He had been a fire direction officer on his previous two firebases, the officer who determines the coordinates for the howitzers during a fire mission. Commanding was actually less compli-cated than being the FDO, but he found he had to think of more issues, one of which was a nagging concern about the tree line that ran away from the firebase to the East. If this little unit would ever be actually attacked by Viet Cong, it would be from that tree line.

He brought the subject up with the first sergeant one morning. They were sitting on their cots in the CO bunker. "Does that East perimeter bother you? I know there's not much activity in this area, but the VC could get so close to us in that treeline."

"Sure it does. But the engineers are down to three dozers for all of the Pleiku region. We're low on the list."

"Do we have any beehive rounds?"

"Lieutenant, the 155 doesn't have a beehive round. I forgot you were with 105 units."

Jacob said, "Oh, yeah. Of course." The 'beehive' round was essentially a shell filled with tiny finned darts. It was aimed directly at an invading enemy, and used only as a last resort. The beehive would have made Jacob more at peace about the East perimeter, but there was none for the 155 howitzer because it used a different type of artillery shell than the 105mm.

"Well," Jacob said. "Let's think . . . "

WHAM!

The first sergeant jumped up. "Incoming!"

Jacob was first out the doorway. Incoming usually meant mortars.

But the explosion wasn't a mortar shell.

A soldier was standing near the communications mast with a grenade launcher in his hands. Smoke and dust were rising from the wreckage of the latrine. Men were running over from the guns and from the bunkers. Jacob noticed some of them were grinning.

The first sergeant cursed up a storm. "Stache, put that down! Now!"

Jacob yelled, "Anybody hurt?!" It seemed impossible that no one would have been hit by shrapnel.

The soldier slowly put the grenade launcher on the ground at his feet. When Jacob got to him, the man seemed dazed. He was wearing a filthy set of fatigues with the sleeves rolled down. He was short and stocky, but his face was oddly thin, almost emaciated. He had a huge, non-regulation mustache.

He turned to Jacob with a vacant look and quietly said, "Hello, sir." Then he began to slowly walk toward one of the bunkers. The first sergeant stopped him and called to one of the gun captains. "Sergeant Tyler, take Stache to your bunker. Tell two of your men to stay with him. Don't let him move an inch."

An angry-looking first sergeant walked back to Jacob. "Okay, sir, this will take some explaining."

"What on earth's going on here? Who *is* that man!"

The first sergeant said, "That's Stache. He's our biggest drughead. I think somebody put him up to it. There was no one in the latrine. They'd make sure of that."

Back in the Command bunker, First Sergeant LaFleur looked genuinely angry. "Here's the thing, Lieutenant. Stache is our biggest problem, but he's also kind of a genius at keeping our generators going. We've got three 5K's and two 10K's, and we're seriously dead without them."

"Is that why I didn't see him on the gun crews?"

"Yeah. He's probably the oldest private in the Army. He was a sergeant but got busted three times for drugs."

"So, what do we do with him? That's a court martial offense, and obviously, we can't demote him any further."

First Sergeant shook his head. "I don't know. That was dangerous. But I think we'd have some real generator problems if we lost him." Then he gritted his teeth, and said, "He even brought one of the 10K's with him when he came to the firebase. In a blue truck. If you scratch the green paint on that 10K, it's blue paint underneath."

"You mean it's an Air Force generator . . . "

"Yes, sir."

"What happened to the truck?"

"Well, we never asked. It was gone a few hours later. But I know there's a kind of valley about two clicks from here where stuff goes." He paused. "So I've been told."

Billy, the radio operator. stuck his head in the doorway. "Two messages from HQ, sir, and Doc Yoder is here. About Stache."

"Good," the first sergeant said. Then he yelled, "Come in, Doc!"

Specialist Yoder was the medic. Although he'd met the medic briefly during the first-day tour of the firebase. Jacob hadn't spoken with him. Yoder was tall, slim, and somewhat surprising to Jacob, handsome. Jacob never thought of GI's as good looking. Dark hair, green eyes, and sunburned. He stood just inside the doorframe, not really at attention, but stiff. He was visibly nervous.

"Sir, First Sergeant, can I talk with you about Stache and what happened?"

"Sit down, Doc," said the first sergeant, "Was anybody hurt?"

"No, First Sergeant. I checked. The latrine pretty much took the whole thing." Yoder looked decidedly uncomfortable. "Sir, I feel like this was mostly my fault. I've been trying to keep an eye on Stache. He's usually not even up by this time."

"Did someone put him up to this?" Jacob asked.

"I don't know, sir. I know he's still drugged out, and he's pretty bad off when he is, but it just doesn't seem like something Stache would do, or think of."

"But he did."

"Yes, sir."

Jacob thought for a moment. It struck him as unusual for a medic to feel so responsible for one of the men. "Specialist," Jacob said kindly, "I appreciate you saying it's your fault; I don't think it is, but I'm glad you're talking to us about this, because we've got a big problem what to do with this man."

"Yes, sir. Stache is scared. I don't think he even knows why he did it, but he knows it means a court martial. He's scared he'll be sent back to base camp in Pleiku. He dreads that." Doc Yoder hung his head for a few seconds, then looked up at Jacob with a sad, distressed look. "Sir, can I tell you what I think is going on?"

"I wish you would." Jacob glanced at the first sergeant, and wondered why he hadn't asked Yoder anything. Then Jacob realized he probably knew a lot of what Yoder was going to say.

"Stache is so deep into drugs, heroin, I don't think he can ever get clean, and he knows it. He's here to die, sir. There's a black market in every village and the stuff is so strong, almost pure . . . and he's been on it so long . . . "

"What do you mean, 'he's here to die'? That's kind of extreme, isn't it?"

Yoder said, "What I mean is that Stache sees this firebase as the place he can be safe and live until he overdoses."

"Good grief, Yoder! Do you think that too?

"Yes, sir."

Jacob sighed. "So what do we do with him? What's your thoughts?"

"Move him into my bunker. I'll watch him, and have both Tyler and Washington join me in making sure he doesn't do something again."

Jacob asked, " They're the two gun captains?"

"Yessir, and they've agreed to help . . . if you give your approval."

Jacob turned to the first sergeant. "What do you think, First Sergeant?"

"Well, sir, there's no really good solution to this, but I think this is the best plan we've got," the first sergeant said. "And we get to keep our generators running," he added, expressing what was clearly on his mind.

Jacob leaned forward and looked hard at the medic. "There's one thing more I want to know. Why are you willing to get involved like this?"

Doc Yoder said very quietly, "I'm trying to save him, sir."

" I thought you said he'd never get clean. "

"Not that kind of saved, sir." Yoder paused. "I think First Sergeant understands."

It was difficult for Jacob to keep a sarcastic tone out of his voice. "You mean religiously."

"Yes, sir."

"Are you also a chaplain, Specialist Yoder?" Jacob asked.

"No, sir. Just a Christian."

"So before he dies on our firebase, you want him to get saved."

"Yes, sir."

Jacob stood up. What a strange situation, he thought. This is crazy. "Okay, Specialist Yoder. I agree to your plan. I'm counting on you and Tyler and Washington to do your best. But I also want you to know that I don't hold you responsible for anything that happens. It's my decision and my responsibility. Is that understood?"

Yoder looked surprised. So did the first sergeant. "Yes, sir," said Yoder.

The weeks went slowly by on LZ Polly. Jacob had Doc Yoder report to him twice a week regarding Stache. Jacob didn't like to admit it, even to himself, but he looked forward to the times of conversation with Yoder. Though Yoder had obviously stated he was religious, he didn't bring it up with Jacob, unless Jacob asked him questions about what he believed and why.

Jacob, a humanities major in college, had a skeptical attitude about all things religious. To Jacob's thinking, religious belief arose from one or more of three things: having been raised as a child to believe, having a superstitious nature attracted to mystical concepts, or having a weakness of character that welcomed the sense of security religion provided.

Yet in these weeks that followed the latrine explosion—causing a renaming of the firebase to 'LZ No Potty'— Jacob became aware of the high regard the men had for Doc Yoder. The next time Yoder came to report how Stache was doing, Jacob somewhat nervously asked him about his religion. 'Well, he's the one who brought it up about saving Stache,' Jacob thought.

"Specialist Yoder, what'd you mean that you thought First Sergeant would understand, when you mentioned Stache and religion?"

Yoder said, "First Sergeant is Catholic, and he and I have talked about how we were both brought up in church. Of course, there are differences, but we have a lot in common."

Jacob was aware that he could well be getting into an inappropriate conversation between an officer and an enlisted man. But he had a sense that Yoder would not see it as familiarity, or take advantage of it. So Jacob, with an apologetic tone, said, "Do you both see growing up religiously as the reason why you believe in God?"

"Good question, sir. I guess I'd say, 'Yes and No.'" Yoder thought for a moment. "I grew up in church, and I don't think I ever *didn't* believe. But I did think it all through years later, when I was about 17. Then I chose to believe it for myself."

Jacob said. "Okay. Ah, I have this theory why people are religious—no offense."

Yoder said seriously, "Of course not, sir. I'd like to hear your thoughts."

Jacob quickly shared his three ideas.

Surprisingly, Yoder nodded his head several times. "I'm impressed, sir. You've really thought about this. I agree with you. I certainly fit into the first category, but not the second two. I'm sure not superstitious."

"But you don't feel a sense of comfort in being religious? Really?"

Yoder smiled and said, "Well, again, it's sort of yes and no. In some ways, I think being a Christian makes life harder, because . . ."

Someone outside was yelling. "*Bac si! Bac si!*"

Yoder jumped up. "Sorry, sir. That's me." He left the CO bunker and walked quickly out toward the village wire gate. An older woman was standing at the gate, calling again and again, "*Bac si! Bac si*"

Jacob knew this was the Vietnamese word for doctor. He followed Yoder. The woman was saying something more in Vietnamese, which neither

Jacob or Yoder could understand. On impulse, Jacob said loudly, "*En Francais!*" He thought, 'she's old enough; maybe she speaks French.'

The woman cried out a long phrase, most of which was incomprehensible for Jacob's high school French. But he heard three words he did know. *Garcon . . . le bras . . . couper.*

He said to Yoder, "She says a boy has cut his arm."

Yoder looked startled. "You speak French, sir?"

"A little. Not much."

"I'll be right back." Yoder ran to his bunker and came running back with his canvas medic's bag. "May I go with her, sir?"

"Of course." Then Jacob said, "I'll go with you."

It seemed like the medic wasn't sure about an officer going with him to the village. Yoder went at least once a week to treat anyone hurt or sick in the village, and he never took a weapon or wore his helmet. "Okay. Thanks, sir. All right if we go just like we are?"

Again, Jacob said, "Of course. Best way."

The village was less than a quarter mile from the firebase. They skirted the rice paddies that edged right up to the village houses. Most of the little dwellings were traditional stick and thatch, but the one the older woman led them to was a ramshackle construction of large scraps of plywood and metal sheets. The roof was corrugated metal held down with large stones.

A young woman was sitting at the door of the house with a little boy in her arms. She had his arm held away from his body. The boy was crying. The woman looked at the older woman anxiously, and the older woman said, "*Bac si.*"

Jacob guessed the boy was five or six years old, and the cut on his arm was about three or four inches long and looked deep.

Yoder knelt down and merely glanced at the wound. He nodded and smiled at the woman and the little boy. He dug a lollipop out of his sack, pulled the cellophane wrapper off, and gave it to the boy. The little boy stuck it in his mouth and stopped crying a bit, but sobbed quietly even with the lollipop in his mouth.

Jacob asked, "Where on earth did you get lollipops?"

Yoder said, "My church sends them to me." He took a small bottle, gauze and a suture kit out of his sack, then asked Jacob, "Sir, could you tell them to hold the boy firmly. I've got to clean and suture that cut. I'll do it super fast, but it's going to hurt and scare him."

Jacob racked his brain for the French word for 'hold.' Amazingly, he remembered. "*Madame*," Jacob addressed the older woman, "*tiens le garcon*." And Jacob pantomimed a firm grip. He also motioned for the older woman to turn the boy's head away so he couldn't see what Yoder was going to do.

Both women held the boy, and Yoder said, "Sir, take his hand and really hold tight, so he won't pull away from me." Yoder put suture thread into just one of the curved needles.

What happened next astonished Jacob. Yoder poured an antiseptic liquid into the cut, cleaned it with the gauze, squeezed the cut closed with one hand and put four sutures in, all in a matter of less than a minute. 'Unbelievable!' Jacob thought.

"Doc . . . that was fast!"

The little boy howled and the lollipop dropped out of his mouth.

Yoder put a bandage on the wound and wrapped it tightly with adhesive tape. "Putting a tight bandage on lessens the pain, " he said. "Not sure why." Then he got another lollipop from the canvas sack and gave it to the boy.

"That's called a running stitch," Yoder said. "It's quick and easy to do. Oh, and this is really good; the bandage is saturated with an antibiotic. It was a pretty clean cut, so I don't think it'll get infected." He handed the older woman a small bottle of aspirin. "Tell them two a day. Morning and evening. And that I'll come back tomorrow."

Jacob pointed to the bottle and said, "*Deux. Per diem*." Then he thought, 'Good grief. That's Latin.' He smiled. "*Deux. A jour. Matin et soir*." The older woman nodded.

Jacob held his hand toward Yoder. "*Bac si. A demain*."

Both women bowed their heads to Yoder. "*Cam on. Cam on. Cam on*," the boy's mother said, with tears on her face. "*Merci, Monsieur le docteur*," the other said very formally.

Later that day, Jacob realized that was the first time he had called Yoder, "Doc."

*

Jacob learned on his first day at LZ Polly, that the Lt. Tillinghast, who was the Fire Direction Officer, was indeed the Officer Candidate School tormentor. When Jacob stopped at the Fire Direction Center to meet the fire direction crew, Lt. Tillinghast, the same short, pudgy upperclassman from OCS, was visibly nervous when he greeted Jacob. "Jacob Saith, seems like a long time since OCS!"

Jacob shook his hand and asked him to introduce the other men on the FDC team.

The nervousness of Tillinghast showed when he actually said, "Yes, sir." Lieutenants never called each other 'sir.' That Jacob now outranked Tillinghast was due simply to the fact that Tillinghast had spent eight months in Germany doing paperwork, and so was still a second lieutenant. Jacob had come directly to Viet Nam from OCS and had quickly been promoted to first lieutenant. In 1969, the shelf life of a lieutenant in Viet Nam was not lengthy.

That evening Jacob thought through on how to relate to Tillinghast. He remembered clearly Tillinghast's harassment of the last three months of Officer Candidate School. It was meant to humiliate. There were only a few upperclassmen who tormented others, but Tillinghast was the worst of the lot. Jacob could also remember imagining ways to get revenge, usually involving an image of a brutal, post-graduation fist-fight.

Jacob realized that Lt. Tillinghast might be expecting some kind of payback for the OCS days. But Jacob became aware, oddly but gratefully, that all he cared about was that the FDC operated well and with speed.

So the following day, Jacob headed over to the FDC. "Let's go see if there's any coffee in the mess tent, lieutenant," Jacob said to Tillinghast.

There was no coffee, and they stood outside the mess tent to talk. Jacob smiled. "What's your first name? I had a name for you in OCS, but it's not one you'd like."

"It's Rick."

"Okay, Rick. Here's the deal. OCS is over and done. Now we need to get the FDC running well, and you and I are both going to spend time this week making sure of that. A big part of that is that the FDC crew sees you and I are a good team. Agreed?"

Tillinghast said, with obvious relief. "Yes. Thanks. I get your point."

"Okay, I was the FDO on my last two firebases. So follow my lead here. I'm guessing you don't remember much from OCS on running a Fire

Direction Center, so we're going to start from scratch. With the night fire programs.

"First of all, move your firing chart over on the board. The center pin is loose and that means you can't measure distances accurately. Second, I see there's a FADAC computer. Don't ever use its data for a fire mission. Use the data the guys get from the slide rules."

Jacob said quietly, "Rick, this is serious stuff. If you don't know something, ask. Not when the men are listening, but ask. I give us four days for the FDC to be able to handle anything."

Jacob smiled again, and held his hand out to Tillinghast. "We can get this done."

In the following five days, Jacob was pleased to see Rick Tillinghast learn the procedures of the FDC quickly and well. He had an excellent memory for details. Jacob went each night, after orienting the three guns of the battery, for the routine night fire programs. Unlike a fire mission called in by ground troops, the night fire programs needed no new computations, so Lt. Tillinghast just oversaw what the FDC crews had been doing for months.

On the fifth day, Jacob called a practice fire mission with the whole crew. There was one 'chart operator' who plotted the coordinates, two 'data guys' who determined the azimuth and elevation numbers for the guns, and Billy, the radio man who radioed the numbers to the gun captains. There was also the somewhat bored operator for the FADAC computer—a bizarre trunk-sized machine made by Magnavox that ran on a 5K generator—that was amazingly slow to determine the same numbers the slide rule guys got quickly. 'Whatever you do a lot, you get good at,' Jacob thought as he watched the data guys do their amazing thing.

The practice mission went really well, and both Jacob and Lt. Tillinghst breathed a sigh of relief.

But the funny incident that welded the FDC team together came the following week. Jacob was in the FDC at the time, and Billy announced a Red Haze fire mission he'd just received from battalion in Pleiku. Red Haze meant an Army aircraft with heat detecting sensors had flown over an area and had picked up a lot of heat. This usually meant Viet Cong troops or machinery.

Billy excitedly gave the coordinates to the chart operator, who almost immediately laughed. "It's us . . ." he said, and pointed at the center pin on the chart. It was the location of LZ Polly. The Red Haze plane had picked up the heat of the firebase at night, and sent it in as a fire mission.

"Battalion plotter is gonna catch it!"

Jacob asked Rick, "What are your orders for this fire mission, Lt. Tillinghast?"

Rick smiled and quietly said, "Billy, tell HQ we cannot comply to Red Haze as we are unable to point our howitzers straight up."

The team loved it and laughed. The FDC was bonded.

*

Jacob often went to the village with Doc Yoder, partly because keeping contact with the older French-speaking woman gave Yoder a way to communicate he hadn't had before, and partly because it gave Jacob a chance to talk with Yoder away from the firebase.

Returning from the village one day, Jacob asked Doc Yoder a question he thought was probably unfair. But it was one Jacob had always wanted to ask a religious person.

"Doc, since you can't see God, how do you know a God even exists?"

"Ah . . ." Yoder didn't say anything for a moment, but he didn't seem annoyed at the question. He looked calm, but then Yoder usually looked calm.

"Lieutenant, that's a hard question. I'm not sure I can answer that. I won't say 'I just know it.' because that's what my father said when I asked him once, and it didn't help."

They were almost at the firebase, and Yoder stopped walking. "I know you're not asking if there's some proof like if somebody has an x-ray of God. So probably the best I can do is tell you why I believe God exists." Then Yoder asked, "Is it okay if I think about that a while?"

Jacob was surprised. "Sure, take your time." He always assumed religious people had ready answers for everything.

As Doc pulled open the wire gate, they both noticed a scruffy tan dog had followed them from the village. It was the skinniest dog Jacob had ever seen. The mongrel's rib cage was pathetic to see.

Doc said, "Oh, that's so sad. I've seen that dog before. He looks terrrible." Then Doc Yoder gave Jacob a look that probably many kids had given their parents.

Jacob laughed. "I know what you're going to ask! Can you keep him? Sure, why not."

"Thanks, sir. I'll give him to Stache to take care of. Maybe good for Stache, and definitely good for the poor dog."

So that's how the friendship began between Private Stache and the dog, whom Stache named 'Corporal.' Stache told Doc Yoder, "I couldn't respect a dog who didn't outrank me."

It was heartwarming to see Corporal gain weight and look healthier every day. Stache adored the dog, and the men were glad to have this happy creature in their midst. Corporal made the rounds of the gun crews every day and ran in crazy, joyous circles when he got food from the men. Corporal gave a small sense of normalcy to this grim little community.

Doc Yoder did get back to Jacob a few days later about Jacob's question. "You've made me work hard, sir!" Yoder said. "I've been looking at my Bible to try to think of the best way to say what I believe."

They were sitting on the low sandbag berm of Gun 3, and Doc Yoder said, "First of all, Lieutenant, I think you're probably smarter than me, so some of this might sound pretty unconvincing to you. For me, God is more real than this sandbag I'm sitting on, but I know my feeling that doesn't prove anything."

"Doc, I don't doubt for a second that you believe strongly. I'm not trying to give you a hard time."

"Oh, I know that, sir! I think your question is really important. Actually, no one's ever asked me that before. It's made me think."

Yoder took a deep breath. "Okay, here goes. Here's why I believe God is real.
Is it okay if I read these parts of the Bible?"

"Well," Jacob said, "To tell the truth, I'd rather you just say it in your own words, but use the Bible if you want."

"Thanks." Yoder took a much-battered Bible from his canvas bag. "Well, the first reason I have is when my mother died, I began to be really afraid of dying too. That probably sounds strange for a young guy, but my mom was only 38. She died of cancer and it was terrible."

Jacob said, "I'm sorry, Doc. How old were you?"

"Seventeen. That's when I began to believe in God for myself." Yoder opened his Bible and read, *I sought the Lord, and He heard me, and delivered me from all my fears.*

"It was just like that and just that fast, sir. I wasn't afraid any more."

Jacob didn't say anything, but he assumed if a person believed something strongly enough, it would have the same psychological effect. Yoder didn't want to be afraid, and felt it was God who took the fear away. 'But, hey,' Jacob thought, 'whatever works.'

"Ok, sir, here's the next one. *The evidence of the Spirit of God is love, joy, peace, patience, kindness . . .* " Doc closed the Bible. "The idea here is that people's lives will change in good ways as they get closer to God. He changes them. For me the big ones were love and kindness." Yoder shook his head. "I was so selfish, and not kind at all to my family."

Jacob said, "Well, everybody's selfish, I guess. I see that as self-survival."

Yoder said seriously, "A month after I got married, my wife, Jenny, told me if I wasn't nicer to her, things were going to be tough. I asked God to help me be kinder to her."

"You're married!?"

Yoder grinned. "Yes, sir. And I have a three-year-old daughter."

"What? Doc, I didn't know that!"

Doc shook his head a little. "It seemed almost unnatural for me to be kind, insecure as I was, so again, I think it was God who helped me. But it wasn't some magical thing. I'd started to read the Bible every day to learn more about God, and I began to pray for Jenny and Annie, not just me."

Jacob felt a sense of uneasiness. In the weeks following Doc's suturing the boy's cut arm, Yoder had asked Jacob lots of questions about his family, where he grew up, what he studied in college—all kinds of things from his past—and Jacob had enjoyed sharing. Yoder was a great listener.

But Jacob suddenly realized the he hadn't really asked much about Yoder's life. He hadn't even known that Doc Yoder was married.

"Were you drafted, Doc? Couldn't you get an exception because of your family?"

"I wasn't drafted. I enlisted and asked for medic training at Sam Houston, sir." Yoder said, "Actually, my family's religion can qualify for conscientious objector status. But I felt God wanted me to enlist."

"So you could save people? Was that what you were thinking?"

"Yes, sir."

Neither spoke for a moment. Then Doc said, "My other reason for believing God exists is that I think He makes every person feel they're worthwhile, no matter how many problems they have, or how bad they act."

"Doc, I don't know about that. There are some pretty lousy people. You think they like who they are?"

"Yeah, I know. This one's hard for me to put in words. I think it's that people just want to be who they are. Yes, sir, there sure are some bad people, and I don't know what they think about themselves or God. But this is the way the Bible puts it for a lot of people . . . *I am carefully and wonderfully made . . . and my soul knows it very well.*

"I don't think it means that they don't wish they were different somehow. In high school, I wished I was smarter, or better at sports. But I never wished I was a different person. I like that it says, '*my soul* knows it very well.' Maybe not my brain, but my soul does." Doc paused. "Does that make sense?"

Jacob thought about himself. Did he feel some unique value for himself? He'd always been a very self-confident person, and wasn't sure he'd ever even thought about whether he liked who he was. So Jacob threw out this question.

"What about people who commit suicide? They don't seem to have a great self value."

"I don't know, sir. I wonder. I guess Stache is almost like a person who's headed for suicide in a way, but I think even he feels he's a worthwhile person in his heart."

Then Doc Yoder asked a question out of the blue. "Have you read much of the Bible, sir? "

Jacob smiled. "Actually, in high school, I tried to once. There was this girl I really liked, Kathy Stevens, who went to church, and she told me I should read the Bible. I started at the beginning, and didn't last too long. I mostly remember that it said God was sorry he'd made people, so he drowned them all."

Yoder groaned. "Oh, man!"

"Sounded like God made a mistake," Jacob said sarcastically, "but somehow didn't know it till it went bad. So he killed everybody off."

Doc had to laugh. "I'm guessing that the girl wasn't too impressed with that."

"I think I was smart enough not to tell her."

"Well, there's a big word my pastor would know for when the Bible makes it seem like God regrets something," Yoder said. "But I think if God's smart enough to create people, He's probably not surprised at what they do. Sad maybe, but not surprised."

"Anyway, that's what I've read of the Bible."

Doc Yoder looked like he was going to say something more, but didn't. "I'd better go see how Stache and Corporal are doing," he said. "Thanks for letting me share my thoughts, Lieutenant."

*

Life on LZ Polly continued in its daily and nightly routine. It was one of utter sameness from day to day, always with the thought that something intense could happen suddenly. Jacob thought back to when he'd played goalie on an inter-mural soccer team. It was exciting for him when the other team was taking shots on his goal, but that also meant his team wasn't doing a very good job on defense, and was probably losing. Life on the LZ was like that. You hated the boredom, but you'd never consciously want the kind of excitement where people could get hurt.

Christmas came and went. The men of Gun 2 made a Christmas tree out of part of a communication mast, with wires stretched to the sides and some spent brass from M16 rifles strung as decorations. Gun 1's crew had taken fake pictures of themselves pretending to cook Campbell's Pork and Beans over an open fire, with only perimeter wire in the background. They'd sent a picture to the Campbell's Company, and suggested that it would be patriotic of Campbell's to ship them cartons of food to LZ Polly, via Pleiku. The Campbell's Company actually did so, and boxes of all kinds of food began arriving, until battalion HQ in Pleiku put a stop to it.

Then one afternoon in mid-January, Billy showed up at the CO bunker with a note. It was a directive from battalion that Billy had taken the trouble to write out. "This is bad, sir," Billy said, and handed Jacob the commo slip. Billy's note said: *Ref. rabies Plei Marong, all units, 1st Bat / 42nd Arty / animal pets not allowed. Animals on bases to be destroyed.*

Jacob read the note carefully. There was no loophole here.

"Sir?" Billy said.

Jacob handed the note to the first sergeant.

"Sir, this is going to kill Stache!" Billy was visibly distressed.

Jacob said, "That's all, Billy. Thank you."

Billy took a step toward the bunker door.

"Wait, Billy!"

Billy turned around.

Jacob said, "Okay, Billy. We're not going to follow through on this directive."

"Oh, God, thank you, sir. And—I don't think we ever really received this message. The radio's been pretty bad lately."

Jacob said, "No, no, Billy. I want you to acknowledge this directive, and that you handed it in person to LZ Polly's CO." He added, "And Billy . . . ?"

"Yes, sir?"

"Make sure you tell Stache and Doc they've got to get Corporal hidden whenever they hear a chopper. Even if it's just slicks delivering food."

"I will, sir. Sir, . . . I'm glad."

Jacob turned to the first sergeant. "First Sergeant . . . ?"

"Interesting, sir. Interesting.."

The next day at noon, Billy came to the CO bunker with a cup of coffee for Jacob. Jacob had been up most of the night with Lt. Tillinghast running an interdiction fire mission: artillery shells hurled out into the night every ten minutes as if to say to the Viet Cong, 'We're here. Behave yourselves.'

Billy had never done such a thing before. Jacob thanked him, but asked, "How do we still have coffee?"

Billy said, "Oh, cook was glad to make extra. There's still some left too, if you want." As Billy left, First Sergeant laughed and said, with a wry smile, "Ah, Lieutenant, the whole base knows about the dog. Billy spread the word. You might actually be the only popular lieutenant in Viet Nam. For the moment, anyhow."

"Well, First Sergeant, I may get court-martialed, but at least I'll have more coffee for a while."

"And you even have a nickname. First I've ever heard of such a thing. Ramirez on Gun 2 gave it to you."

"I'm afraid to ask."

The first sergeant said, "I think it's okay, even a compliment, sort of. It's El T."

"LT? That's not really a nickname."

"No, not LT, like your rank. It's El, like the Spanish word for 'the.' And T. So it's 'The T.'"

Jacob had no idea what it meant.

Then the first sergeant said very seriously, "I think this is actually good for morale."

"Okay, thanks, First Sergeant."

Then Jacob added. "I'm glad you're on this firebase, First Sergeant."

First Sergeant LaFleur looked a bit uncomfortable. "Yes, sir."

Jacob took a chance and asked the first sergeant a personal question. "First Sergeant, I don't even know your first name."

One word, with a smile and shake of the head. "Napolean."

"Really! That's great."

"My family's French Canadian," First Sergeant said. "It wasn't much fun as a kid, believe me. And before you ask, no, I don't speak much French."

Then changing the subject, the first sergeant asked, "Is it still good for me to go into Pleiku this week, Lieutenant? I need to meet with S4 about fuel. And there's a warrant officer who was with a self-propelled 155 unit. I think I could learn something from that man."

"Sure. Just don't mention dogs."

A few days later, Jacob was walking past the generator pit, where Stache was working on a 10K, with Corporal lying close by. Jacob called out over the noise, "The dog looks really good! You've helped him a lot."

Stache looked at Jacob. It was the only time Jacob had spoken to Stache. He didn't smile. Doc Yoder had mentioned that long-term heroin use did not make for nice smiles. Stache yelled, "Lieutenant, thank you for what you did."

"I like dogs too." Jacob yelled back.

Eight days later a terse message came from battalion. It said: *Directive ref. rabies alert / countermanded.*

Jacob was angered and saddened. There may have been a time when he would have found this funny, and joked about 'the right way, the wrong way, and the Army way.' But now he could only think about soldiers on battalion firebases all over the Central Highlands who had shot their pet dogs, and were grieved to do it. 'This stinks so bad,' he thought.

Then it suddenly hit him. What had led him to openly disobey that directive? It hadn't seemed like a big deal at the time to tell Billy, "We're not going to do that," and it *had* seemed like a terrible thing to kill Corporal. He certainly hadn't made that quick decision to win favor from the men. Jacob was one of those people who didn't think much about whether people liked him or not.

All he could think was that it was what Doc would've done . . . or would have silently wanted Jacob to do. Doc would probably gladly get himself in trouble if it meant he could help someone he cared about. And Doc seemed to care about a lot of people.

And the outcome—the strange countermanded directive—gave Jacob an odd sense that it was meant to be.

First Sergeant LaFleur returned from Pleiku with interesting news. He had talked with the warrant officer who had been with a SP artillery unit. SP, or Self-Propelled, artillery meant a howitzer was mounted in what was basically a tank. It was armor-plated and, like a tank, was on motorized tracks that made it mobile.

"Turns out there *is* a beehive round for the 155. Some of the SP units tried them. They were called Killer Junior, but it's basically a beehive," First Sergeant said.

"How'd they do it?" Jacob asked.

"It's pretty simple, actually. You use a regular HE round, with a charge one powder bag, the fuse set at one second and an elevation of 15 mils. It'll go out about 50 meters or so, and explode 30 feet off the ground." First Sergeant added, "The WO said it was unlike anything he'd ever heard, it was that loud."

"A high explosive shell at 50 meters. Good grief!"

Jacob tried to picture this mentally. "So why don't units like ours use this, or even know about it?"

"Well," First Sergeant said, "the big problem is that the shrapnel coming back is pretty bad. The SP guys didn't care because they were in their vehicle. But a firebase is so exposed, the blow-back could hit our guys as well as the VC."

"Yeah, but we've got the tree line a lot closer than 50 meters. The shell would go into the trees and wouldn't that kill the shrapnel coming back?" Jacob paused. "Since it's a timed fuse, not a contact detonator, it won't explode until it's well into the trees."

The first sergeant took a moment to answer. "I think you're probably right about that, Lieutenant. The other problem is obviously we're not a tank, so the guys would have to jack down one of the guns onto the speed jack every night. It's such a low charge, you can fire this thing off the speed jack, so it's easy to point the gun anywhere, but it's a lot of work to do every night."

Jacob said, "I don't think we'd even need to worry about aiming. The East perimeter is the only target. Leave it on the firing jack, and have the gun crews take turns being the beehive gun."

"Okay, I can see that," the first sergeant said. "The only other issue is the guys would have to punch the shell out of the tube the next morning. You know how they hate that. Of course it won't explode, but it's nervous for the men to be banging away on the nose of the shell."

Jacob nodded. Using a long ramrod, the men would have to forcefully push the shell out of the breech from the gun's muzzle.

Neither man spoke for a minute. This idea took a lot of thinking about. Both Jacob and the first sergeant would have been hard put to declare then and there if this were a solution to a problem, or a new problem.

Jacob said, "Let's give this a lot of thought." And he added, "and obviously, we won't mention anything to the gun crews until we decide."

A few days later, LZ Polly had an extended fire mission called in by an American officer serving with a unit of Vietnamese irregulars, called, for some reason, Ruff Puffs. It was a 'chase' mission, following a Viet Cong company with artillery. It lasted for thirty-five minutes, and both the FDC and the gun crews got a real workout. The gun crews probably complained, but in reality loved it, because a long fire mission gave them a chance to get into a rhythm.

And while the official training for the 155 loading procedure specified two men holding a loading tray with the shell on it, and one more man with a rammer, in real life, it was simpler and faster. The biggest, strongest man on the gun just lifted the 100 pound shell, balanced it on his left hand, made a fist at the back of the shell and rammed it into the gun's breech by sheer force. The powder man threw the bags of gunpowder in, the breech was closed, and the gun fired in as little as fifteen seconds.

During the Ruff Puff mission, the gun crews pumped out nearly four rounds a minute.

There is satisfaction in doing anything well, including being a soldier. While artillery-men in Viet Nam were not in the degree of danger as the infantry, they were still in a combat zone, and they took pride in the skills needed to fire the big guns.

After the mission, Jacob went to the FDC and complimented the men and Lt. Tillinghast on a good mission. As he left the Fire Direction Center, Tillinghast walked out with him.

"Jacob, I just wanted to apologize for being such a jerk to you in OCS," he said. Tillinghast had the anxious expression he had on their first LZ Polly meeting.

"Ah, well . . . " Jacob said, "That's okay. But what was that about? Why'd you do that?"

"That's easy," Tillinghast said. "I was always the fat kid growing up. I got bullied in school, and OCS was my chance to bully someone else. I guess that sounds pretty pathetic."

Jacob had to laugh. "Actually, that makes sense. And it's kind of funny. Hopefully, that's out of your system now."

Rick Tillinghast said seriously. "Man, when First Sergeant told me you were going to be the CO for Polly, I was living in dread for a couple of days. I knew you could figure out a way to make my life miserable."

"Ah, well . . ." Jacob said again.

"The fact that you didn't, made me feel ashamed. So, again, I'm sorry about that OCS stuff."

Jacob said with a smile, "The important thing is we've got a good FDC—and a good FDO"

*

Doc Yoder's report on Stache that week was not encouraging. "He loves the dog, and that's helped him mentally. But the heroin use is still really bad. If anything, he's using even more."

"Does he snort it?" Jacob asked.

"Yes, sir."

"I'm amazed he can still work on the generators." Jacob said. "So what do you think the next month or so is going to be for Stache? Is there *anything* you can do to help him?"

Doc Yoder had a curious look on his face, and he said quietly, "Sir, I'm glad that you care about him. I mean, not just because of the generators." Then he added, "And no, there's nothing I know that will help."

Jacob cursed. "Life is hard."

"Yes, sir, it is."

"What did you mean a while back when you said being a Christian made life even harder? Do you remember that?"

" Yes, I sure do."

"So why does being religious make life harder?"

Yoder reached down and took his Bible from his bag. But he didn't open it. He said, "I know you'd rather I say things in my own words, so here goes. In the Old Testament, there was a king, Solomon, who was supposed to be the wisest man alive."

Jacob said, "Is that the deal where he was going to cut the baby in half?"

"Yes, sir! Good memory. Actually, that was just a trick to see who the real mother was. He wasn't really going to cut a baby in half.

"Anyway, Solomon tried to find out what was important in life, and after trying all sorts of things, he decided that there wasn't anything that was really important."

"'Vanity, vanity. All is vanity!'" quoted Jacob dramatically.

'"Aha! You do know some Bible, sir!"

"Well, everybody knows that bit."

"So Solomon decided that everything was meaningless. He even said that if people were smart, and saw life as it really was, they'd have more pain and grief than other people." Yoder added, "Pain at seeing how stupid everything was, I mean."

"Okay. It's extreme, but I get the idea. What's the point with Solomon?"

"The idea is," Yoder said, "that Solomon saw life as it really was, so he couldn't pretend that life was easy or great. He was stuck with the truth about life, and since this is way before Jesus came to earth, there was no answer to give any meaning to life."

Yoder went on. "So I think Christians have the same thing. Once they know truth about life or themselves, they can't pretend anymore, or get distracted from how hard life can be."

"And you think most Christians have this true view of life, as you call it?" Jacob asked, skeptically.

Yoder shook his head. "Actually, no. Unfortunately. But for serious Christians, even though they see how hard life is, they have the—what's the best way to say this—they're sure that God cares about them, and it gives their life meaning. There's a kind of joy in that."

"Again, no offense, Doc, but how on earth could they know that?"

"Well, I see it as peace of mind. Jesus said that in Him we'd have peace, even if we have the kind of trouble Solomon talked about." Yoder paused. "It's hard to say what peace of mind is, but everybody knows it when they feel it. I guess that's the difference between Christians today and Solomon."

"Do you have peace of mind, Doc?'

"Yes, sir, I do."

"Okay," Jacob said. "Give me a one minute explanation of how Jesus fits in."

Doc Yoder smiled and said, "I don't know about one minute, but I can tell you that pretty fast."

"Good, fire away. In your own words."

Yoder said, "I see it this way. Here's three fast Bible statements." He grinned. "Sorry about that. It'll be Bible, but in my words, I promise. First, that if a person is really trying to know about God, he can start off by assuming that God does exist. I mean, even if he doesn't actually believe that, he can at least—how do I say this—kind of seriously pretend God exists in order to try to learn about Him. Does that make sense?"

Jacob said immediately, "Of course. In a philosophy class that's a form of an *a priory* assumption." He laughed at the expression on Yoder's face. "All that means is a starting point. Something I agree to for the sake of argument."

"Yes! Yeah, that's what I mean. And then God says He's glad when someone is trying to understand Him, and He'll reward it."

"What's the reward?"

"That's the second statement. This one will definitely take more than a minute. The Bible says the best way God proves His love for people is that Jesus died for them while they were still sinning."

Jacob frowned. And Yoder added quickly, "That's a religious word, sin, but it just means the selfish, wrong stuff people do."

Jacob said, "Everybody makes mistakes."

"Yes, sir. But sin is more than just mistakes. It means something wrong somebody does on purpose. And Jesus, who never sinned, covers that by paying for it."

"You're saying that Jesus dies because some guy took the last piece of cake? Really?" Jacob said. "Or, the guy goes to hell because he took the cake?" Then he felt uneasy. He hadn't meant to be sarcastic or dismissive of what Doc was sharing. He'd intended to have a calm, hypothetical discussion with Yoder.

But Doc Yoder didn't look offended at all. In fact, he seemed pleased at Jacob's comment. "Lieutenant, you've got a way of asking great questions. I know you remember the little boy in the village with the cut on his arm?"

"Sure. Of course."

"Well, his cut healed, but what if it had gone septic? Even though the rest of him was healthy, that little septic area could have killed him eventually." Here Doc did open his Bible to about the middle, then glanced at Jacob and closed it again. "So even if 99 percent of the boy's body was healthy, the one percent, if it turned to gangrene, would have killed him."

Yoder paused. "That's how God sees sin. It's not that God is harsh. It's just that He's holy, and if I went to God with even a little morally wrong, I'd be like a moth in a blast furnace. Does that make sense?"

Jacob realized this was a favorite comment of Doc's: 'Does that make sense?'

Jacob said, "Okay, I see the logic of what you're saying, at least from the medical angle. But it still seems *so* extreme."

"Yes, sir. But God's view of good and bad isn't like probably a lot of people's. We might think if a person is more good than bad, then the good outweighs the bad. But God sees it like the septic thing, or cancer."

"Okay Doc, I see your point. I'd never heard that before," Jacob said.

"And the third statement," Yoder said quickly, "is that if a person believes this about Jesus, then the Bible says he's a child of God."

"Meaning saved religiously."

"Yes, sir, saved. But to me like it's more of a relationship with God than being part of a religion."

Neither said anything for a few moments. Then Jacob said, "Okay, Doc. Thanks. You did a good job of explaining." Then, as an afterthought, he threw in, "By the way, Doc, when it's just us, you can call me Jacob."

Doc Yoder looked shocked. "Oh, no, sir! I mean, I'm sorry, I know it'd be okay with you, but I just don't think I could do that."

Jacob nodded. "Yeah, okay. I know what you mean." He laughed to lighten the moment. "I'm okay with 'sir.'"

*

Jacob decided to go ahead with the beehive round for one of the howitzers each night. The three guns would take turns. It meant loading the shell and powder after midnight. There'd be no conflict with the night fire programs, since these were fired by only one gun.

The first sergeant gave the news to the gun captains, and Jacob suspected that his brief popularity because of Corporal's reprieve took a hit. He also noticed in the mornings when the gun crews pushed the unused shell back out of the breech, they did so with increasing ease. Jacob knew this meant they weren't ramming the shell into the howitzer with any real force at night. However, the short distance the shell was to travel—and the complete lack of any need for accuracy— made this perfectly okay.

In February came the rain. A rare northeast monsoon event was turning LZ Polly into a two-acre mud puddle. To boredom was now added the depressing misery of being constantly wet.

Sgt. Tyler of Gun 1 came up with an inter-gun athletic competition called the 'Potty Games,' with such events as the sandbag toss, Spam-ball eating contest, and three swimming categories: free style, back stroke, and butterfly. The swimming took place in the space between the mess tent and Gun 3, which was the biggest and deepest expanse of mud and water. The Fire Direction Center team was also invited to participate.

First Sergeant LaFleur was, of course, the referee and judge.

"Swimmers, take your starting positions! For the butterfly!"

"What's a butterfly?" yelled PFC Ramirez from Gun 2.

"You figure it out, Ramirez." First Sergeant yelled back. "On your marks, get set, go!"

And the swimmers were off! Ramirez had obviously not figured out what the butterfly stoke was, as he basically tried to roll through the muddy water toward the finish line.

But little, skinny Billy, from the FDC, of all people, was the star of the butterfly event. He porpoised his way to the finish line, the trails of Gun 3, in spite of a terrific sneezing fit from water up his nose. Admitedly, his only competition was Ramirez, and two huge rammers from Guns 1 and 3, both of whom nearly drowned.

His trophy was a can of Spam with a face drawn on it.

"Swimmers, get ready for the back stroke!" called out First Sergeant.

Jacob was amazed to see the FDC crew pushing Lt. Tillinghast toward the starting line. Tillinghast was laughing, and Jacob was glad to see how the FDC team had taken a liking to Rick Tillinghast.

Seeing Tillinghast flailing away in the muddy water was one of the funniest things Jacob had ever seen.

"I can't see!" hollered Tillinghast, almost submerged. "Where's the finish line!"

All of the gun crews started screaming out different directions. "Sir, turn around! You're headed back to the mess tent!"

"Turn right, sir!"

"You've already won, sir! You can stop!"

All in all, the Potty Games were a huge success. Jacob was impressed that Sgt. Tyler had the idea. It was a good morale boost at a time when it was sorely needed.

A week later, Doc Yoder came to the CO bunker with news about Stache. "Sir, Stache has asked Christ to forgive him."

"Ah . . . " Jacob wasn't quite sure how to respond to this. He could tell from the look on Doc's face that this was of utmost importance. "So Stache is saved. " It wasn't a question.

Doc looked directly at Jacob and said with great seriousness. "Yes, sir. Stache is saved. He's asked the Lord to forgive him and save him." It seemed Doc was intently searching for something from Jacob, a positive reaction or some kind of an acknowledgment that this news was a good thing. But Jacob just said, "Well, that must be a real relief for you, Doc."

"Yes, sir. It means that no matter what happens now, Stache is okay."

Jacob was both skeptical and strangely interested. "What happened? What did Stache say?"

"He told me that he'd always believed in God, but he didn't think Jesus could forgive him for the way he's lived."

"What changed his mind?"

Doc seemed a little embarrassed. "Well, ah, he said it was because if *I* cared about him, and forgave him, it finally hit him that for sure Christ could. So he asked Christ to forgive him."

"Good for you, Doc."

"Sir, could I ask you for a favor?"

"Sure, Doc. You name it."

Yoder said, "Would you be willing to read a part of the Bible? I'd really like to know what you think about it. It's just two chapters, John and Romans."

"Ah, Doc, I don't know about that."

"I can loan you a Bible."

Jacob thought to himself, 'I guess this is the moment of truth.' He said to Yoder, "Listen, Doc, I know you're not trying to talk me into something. And I appreciate that. But I'm just not ready to get into any discussions about the Bible. So I guess I have to say no to your favor."

"Yes, sir. I understand."

"Actually, Doc, I'm not sure you do." Jacob got up and pointed to a plank that served as a bookshelf. "Those are the Army regs for all the procedures of artillery. They're all logical and tested for about a hundred years. They're useful because they make sense. Your explanation of Jesus makes sense too. If every stinking selfish thing people do has to be paid for—and the people can't do it themselves—then the Jesus thing is at least logical. So let's say I'm the opposite of Stache."

Doc nodded. "Okay. But how are you the opposite of Stache?"

"Because while, to me, the Jesus idea makes sense, I still don't really think God exists at all. A smart philosopher could have come up with the concept of Jesus as a good solution for life's problems. Something to give people hope.

"So Stache always believed in God, but didn't know about Jesus. I get the Jesus part, but I honestly don't believe in God."

Jacob couldn't tell from Doc's expression what he thought about this. Doc always appeared so calm. Doc said, "You're honest, sir. Very honest. This is kind of the reverse of you asking me why I believe in God . . . but, why do you *not*?"

Jacob realized a time had come in their relationship, friendship really, when he could share personal thoughts with Doc Yoder. He knew Doc would never take it inappropriately.

"Okay, Doc, sometimes I wake up in the middle of the night, and then I get to thinking about things. Mostly what I remember are regrets or sad things. Like a time when my brother and I were out in the woods with our 22's. A squirrel actually fell out of a tree about three feet from me. It was stunned and just lying there. And I shot it. It didn't really bother me then, but for years I've had the picture in my mind of that squirrel twitching and its legs trying to run before it died. Why did I *do* that?"

Yoder listened quietly. Jacob speaking was with intensity now. "Or in junior high, there was a girl whose mom was poor. There was no dad, which was unusual back then. And this mom wanted her daughter to be like the other kids, and for the other kids to like her. But the girl's clothes were thrift store stuff, and the other kids made fun of her for that."

Doc nodded. "That's sad."

Jacob said, "And there was this thing the school did called 'dessert day,' where kids brought sweets to school to pass around. Mostly they brought in tons of candy bars or cupcakes. But the girl's mom always made these pathetic little weird cookies. So they made fun of her for that too. And no one sat with her at lunch." Jacob added seriously, "I think junior high lunchtime is the cruelest thing ever invented!"

"You thought about that back in junior high? That's pretty compassionate."

"No. That's just it. I didn't. It wasn't until high school, when the other girl, Kathy Stevens, talked to me about God, that I thought about how cruel it was for the girl in junior high. And I hated it that I wasn't nicer to her. I did ask her once why she hadn't told her mom about the cookies, or how bad school was. She just said, 'I love my Mom.'"

Yoder said, "What a kind girl."

"Yeah, she wanted to spare her mother unhappiness. If she could be that kind, why couldn't God be the same, and spare the girl the cruelty. So in high school, I concluded that if there was no God, then the unfairness and cruelty and sadness was just the reality of how life is. I could understand that. I hated it, but I could understand it. What I couldn't understand was if there was a God and he, or it, was okay with how cruel life was, then it just made me angry. I don't want to believe in a god like that."

"Do you still feel that way, sir?"

"Doc, I don't know. I mean it sounds almost childish when I say it, but there's a gut feeling that there's something not right . . . if God does exist. I was glad to get to college where basically no one believed in God. It sure didn't give me a sense of peace, but at least there was no one for me to be mad at."

"Lieutenant, if that's how you see God, as uncaring," Doc said, "I can understand why you wouldn't want to believe in Him. Neither would I." Doc thought for a few seconds then posed a question. "Sir," Doc Yoder said, "Why don't you *ask* God if He exists? Not an uncaring God, but a good God. Really."

"Doc, I can't ask someone I don't believe in if he exists. That doesn't make sense."

"Well, how about that 'a prior' thing you mentioned?"

"That's for the sake of a theoretical discussion. I mean like a philosophical argument. This would mean I believe enough to ask, and I just don't."

"Lieutenant, I've got to tell you, I'm impressed with how you've thought about this. I still say you should ask God to make it clear if He's real, and I believe He will. I just feel that God is somehow getting into your life, and that He wants you to ask anything. We can ask God anything, except one thing . . . the thing Job almost asked."

"What's the one thing?"

"God, are You good?"

*

The attack on LZ Polly started in the early morning of March 27th.

Mortar rounds began coming in about 5 AM, and as Jacob and the first sergeant grabbed their steel helmets and ran out of the CO bunker, they could hear small arms fire as well. Their night guards had begun firing back at the East perimeter tree line at the sound of the first mortar.

There was no need to tell the gun crews an attack was occurring, and most of the men were already firing their M-16 rifles into the darkness. No trip flares had gone off in the perimeter wire. Either sappers had disabled them or the VC were not yet in the wire. Sappers were the nightmare—Viet Cong commandos trained to crawl through razor wire and onto a firebase with explosives.

Jacob yelled to the first sergeant to get the grenade launchers at Gun 3 into action. Jacob ran for the FDC. As he looked back at the first sergeant, he saw him fall to the ground, but then get back up again running.

Jacob stuck his head into the FDC. "Everyone stay here! Get your weapons, but stay here. Billy, let Battalion know!"

"I already have, sir!"

As Jacob ran back out, he heard a lot of small arms. It seemed to him like the nearest howitzer, Gun 1, was leaning at a crazy angle, a wheel blown off, probably from a rocket propelled grenade.

The gun crews were doing a good job. Crouched down behind the sandbag berms, they were pretty well protected from incoming AK-47 rifle fire, and mortars as well. A lot of mortar rounds were coming in.

Someone threw a trip flare into the wire by hand, but the light showed nothing.

Jacob saw a mortar round hit the top of the FDC, but the two feet of dirt and steel plate made it ineffective, though the sound of the explosion inside the FDC must have been tremendous.

'Sappers and rockets,' Jacob thought, 'God, don't let there be sappers!'

Jacob looked toward Gun 2's position, and two things happened simultaneously—the boom of Gun 2 going off, and the flash of a rocket propelled grenade hitting the howitzer almost at the same instant.

Immediately there was a deafening crack. Jacob felt a tingling in his right hand, and in that strange, fast recognition one can have, realized his left eardrum had burst. 'The beehive! Someone fired the beehive!'

Then, all of a sudden, there was relative quiet. There were only the sounds of small arms from his own men.

Jacob ran to Gun 3, and found the first sergeant. He had put two of the gun crews behind the bunker wall and they were firing grenade launchers at the wire. Jacob yelled, "Are you okay?"

First Sergeant LaFleur said, "Nothing much."

"Good. Have the M79 guys hold fire for a minute."

First Sergeant walked slowly to the bunker, holding his side, and spoke to the men, and the grenade launchers stopped.

Jacob saw Sgt. Washington, Gun 3's leader, and asked him, "Sergeant, can you pop an illumination round this close? Charge one, and max elevation?"

"It won't be very close, sir, but I'll do it."

"Even if it's a half click out, it'll help."

The small arms fire from Gun 1 tapered off. Sgt. Tyler had probably ordered this. There was now an almost total silence. Jacob was puzzled. Had the attack ended so soon? That short a conflict was almost unheard of. But even the mortars had stopped. From start to finish, it was less than 20 minutes.

First Sergeant came back, and Jacob said, "First Sergeant, have the M79's fire a grenade every few minustes just past the wire. And let's put some light on the wire and the tree line if we can. Have somebody throw trip flares out there every now and then. We still have an hour till daylight."

Jacob looked around the firebase. "This is unbelievable that it's died down so fast."

"Yes, sir. And Lieutenant, I think your hand is pretty bad. You'd better put a field dressing on that."

For the first time, Jacob looked at this right hand. All four fingers were badly cut, and when he tried to make a fist, two of them didn't move. It was bad, but only a hand. Jacob crouched down and walked quickly toward Gun 2. The illumination round popped overhead about a half-kilometer out, drifting slowly down on its parachute. It gave a dim light to the LZ.

It began raining hard and in the semi-darkness, Jacob didn't see what was lying next to the disabled howitzer until he was a couple of feet away.

"Oh God. Oh, God . . . " It was Doc Yoder and Stache, both dead from terrible wounds. Corporal, the dog, unhurt, was lying tight against Stache's side. Corporal looked at Jacob and whimpered.

"No, no, no." Jacob said out loud. He knelt down and looked at the faces of Stache and his friend, Doc Yoder. And Jacob cried. Corporal came and put his nose under Jacob's left hand. Jacob petted the dog, and cried.

The dawn came with no further action. The two M79 grenade launcher men and five others with M16 rifles went through the village gate outside the perimeter. They cautiously circled around to the tree line. The Viet

Cong were gone. There were no VC bodies visible in the wire at first light. The attack on LZ Polly was over.

Jacob and First Sergeant made sure the base was secure, with guards posted, unusual for daylight. The bodies of Doc Yoder and Stache were brought to the CO bunker, and First Sergeant had the men put Doc on Jacob's cot, and Stache on his own.

First Sergeant had been shot in his side, but he felt a rib had deflected the bullet and that no serious damage had been done. He said, "After 18 years in the Army, I finally get a Purple Heart." He was more concerned with Jacob's hand. But Jacob had said, "It'll keep."

"I'm sorry about Doc and Stache, sir." First Sergeant said quietly. "I really am."

"So am I, First Sergeant."

There had been another soldier badly hurt. It was PFC Peterson from Gun 1. He had been firing his M16 from behind the howitzer when the gun was hit by a rocket propelled grenade. He'd received a serious wound to his abdomen, and he was the first man aboard the dust-off chopper, the medical evacuation helicopter, when it landed just forty minutes after daylight. The next dust-off carried away Doc and Stache, and the first sergeant, who didn't want to go.

"You could have internal bleeding, Get on the chopper. That's an order." Jacob shook hands left-handed with First Sergeant LaFleur and said, "It's been an honor to serve with you, First Sergeant."

"Same here, Lieutenant. Same here." Then he added, "Sir," and saluted. At noon, another helicopter flew in from Battalion. A major and captain came through the supply gate. It was the Battalion executive officer, and Jacob's replacement. The major said, "You'll come back with me, Lieutenant. You've got five minutes to get your gear. Captain Vardman will take over as of now."

Jacob said, "Yes, sir." Then he went to the FDC and said goodbye to Rick Tillinghast and the FDC team. Rick just said, very seriously, "Thank you, Jacob."

The major said little on the way to Pleiku, other than, "I'll see you before you go. I know they're going to send you to Nha Trang to the base hospital, so we'll talk soon."

At the evac hospital in Pleiku, an Army doctor took the field dressing off Jacob's hand, looked at the cut fingers and said, "Eww, nasty . . . " in a casual manner, redressed the wound and braced the back of the hand and wrist with a splint.

Jacob did not look.

The doctor said, "There's an orthopedic surgeon in Nha Trang at the base hospital, and that's where you're headed in about a half hour. Oh, and a major is here to see you before you go. Good luck with the hand!"

Jacob quickly asked, "Captain, I think my left eardrum burst.. Could you take a look."

The doctor grabbed an otoscope and looked. "Yup. It is. But don't worry. Eardrums heal on their own. It'll be okay."

The doctor made Jacob lie down, and the Battalion XO walked in with a clip board.

"Lieutenant Saith, I want to do a fast debriefing on the event last night at LZ Polly."

"Yes, sir," Jacob said. "Sir, if I can ask, do you know how PFC Peterson is doing? He was badly wounded and was evac'd here."

The XO looked at his clipboard. "There were three KIA: a Specialist Jonathan Yoder, Private Harold Talva, and PFC Richard Peterson."

It was what Jacob had dreaded. "So Peterson didn't make it."

"That's correct. There were five injuries, only two listed as serious: yourself and First Sergeant LaFleur. And neither you or the first sergeant are all that serious. The first sergeant is here recovering."

"Yes, sir." Jacob was not surprised at the apparent callousness of the major. Base camp administrative officers lived in a different world, perhaps of necessity.

The XO continued, "First of all, Lieutenant, I have to tell you there'll be no medals given for the incident last night. Well, of course, the Purple Hearts, but nothing else. I understand you used a Killer Junior, or beehive round. Is that right?"

"Yes, sir."

"Were you aware that the beehive is unauthorized for the 155? For this battalion? Because of the possibility of American casulties?"

"No, sir, I wasn't."

The major wrote something on a form. "I'll make a note of that, Lieutenant. You will not be held responsible." He put the clipboard down on the foot of the cot. "Because of the unauthorized nature of the, shall we say, 'defense' weapon employed, the Army has decided to keep the events of last night under wraps. It will be referred to as an incident."

He added, as an attempt to be a little conciliatory, "I have no doubt that using the beehive helped bring the incident to a close. But even so, if we overlooked the use of it for LZ Polly, other LZ's would feel free to use it also, and that we cannot have." He stood up. "Do you have any questions, Lieutenant?"

"No, sir," Jacob said. "None."

"Very well. Your ride to Nha Trang will be at the North helipad in ten minutes. Please be there."

Jacob said, "Yes, sir."

The Battalion debriefing was finished.

The surgery on his hand at the big base hospital in Nha Trang took a long time. Because he had eaten the day before, the doctor used a local anesthetic rather than a general. It was decidedly unnerving for Jacob to have to listen to the surgeon and assistants discuss what they were doing. It was obviously a complex procedure, as two major tendons had been severed. One assistant was clearly in awe of the surgeon's work. "That's beautiful!" he said. "That's just beautiful!"

Jacob was given something to make him sleep, and awakened mid-morning in bed in a huge ward. He had a cast on his right arm from elbow to fingertips. He could see buttons, exactly like shirt buttons, wired to the tips of his ring finger and pinky. The male nurse told him he would have to remain in Nha Trang for at least three weeks, until, as the nurse said, "All the wires come out."

And so began a strange, inactive time for Jacob. He was mobile, and walked around the hospital whenever he could. There were more seriously wounded men than he, and he made a point of talking with them, usually about their families. All these men would be going home when they were able.

As usual, Jacob woke in the early morning hours and thought hard about Doc and Stache. He remembered Doc's saying the one question you couldn't ask God was, 'Are You good?' Jacob thought if God did exist, that's the one question Jacob *would* ask. He kept thinking, 'Is this how you treat people who are trying to serve you, God?' These were hard nights.

One morning, as Jacob was returning from the latrine, he saw someone standing at his bed. 'That is one *big* man!' Jacob thought. The image of a giant in fatigues was reinforced as Jacob got to his bed. Then Jacob saw the man's collar had two stars. 'Oh, my gosh,' he thought, 'a general!'

"Good morning, sir, " Jacob said, and instinctively began to raise his right arm, cast and all, to salute. The giant had a friendly face.

"Don't do that, Lieutenant Saith," the general said. "That's the worst part of my hospital visits; people tend to want to salute or jump up. And probably pull stitches out." He glanced around the ward. "You're obviously able to walk. Is there anywhere we can go that's a bit more private?"

Jacob thought, 'Oh, man, I'm in trouble about something.' He said aloud, "Yes, sir. There's the admin office. I seldom see anyone in there."

"Good. Let's go."

Once in the little office, the general started with, "No, you haven't done anything wrong. I was up in Pleiku talking with an old friend of mine, First Sergeant LaFleur, about you. Oh, and by the way, he's fine, and will stay in Pleiku."

Jacob was shocked. Why would a major general from Division be talking about him? Jacob said, "First Sergeant is a very good man, sir."

"Okay, let me say this straight out. Hold your thoughts. And this conversation is off the record. We think the attack on Polly was a test." He snorted. "Yeah, I know they're going to call it an incident. Stupid. Anyway, you probably wondered why no one came into the perimeter wire. The enemy had no intention of taking the LZ. I think, no, I'm sure, the VC just wanted to see what a 3 gun LZ could put up as a defense.

"I mean, they had to make it look serious, with the mortars and RPG's, but they weren't going to follow through."

"And yet three of our men died."

Unlike the major, the general looked grieved. "Yes, Lieutenant. I'm sorry about those men. I had a captain look into as many details as possible about the attack. I'm especially sad that the medic, Yoder, was due to go home, but he re-up'ed about two weeks ago."

Jacob felt stunned. "I didn't know that, sir. Two weeks ago."

"Yes. I don't know about PFC Peterson, but I do know Stache."

"What! You knew Stache, sir? How?"

"Everybody in the Central Highlands knows about Stache. He's sort of famous." The general paused. "Not always for stellar reasons. The Air Force is convinced he stole a generator from them."

Jacob had to smile, and said, "Yes, sir, he did. It's still on LZ Polly. And I just learned his name was Harold."

"Harold! I never thought of Stache having another name."

The general continued. "Here's what First Sergeant told me about LZ Polly. One, you used a beehive round with the 155 howitzer in a completely unauthorized way. Two, you disobeyed a directive to destroy a pet dog. A directive which was later rescinded, which makes it the second stupidest thing I've ever heard of. Yes, I know . . ."

"Sir . . . "

"And third," the general said seriously, "I'm glad you did both of those. First Sergeant said you're an officer who doesn't mind taking responsibility."

"What? I don't understand."

"Think about it, Lieutenant. If the attack was a test, and I'm pretty sure it was, then the Viet Cong *now* believe that 155 howitzers have a beehive. They never knew that. Most of our own people don't. I'm not saying what you did was right or wrong, but you just may have saved some American lives down the road. Do you know what I'm saying?"

"Yes, sir. Thank you, sir."

"Just so you know, I recommended you for regular Army. If you plan to stay in, that will make a big difference." A pause. "*Do* you plan to stay in?"

"Thanks, Sir, I appreciate your recommendation very much. But I plan to finish up my three years, probably at Sill, then I'd like to find a teaching job."

"Ah, well. If you reconsider, come back and work for me at Division." The general added as an afterthought, "*Did* any shrapnel come back at the base from the beehive?"

Jacob said, "Ironically, I think the only shrapnel that hurt anyone, was my hand. I'm guessing that from the timing."

"Ah, that's poetic." The general stood up

"Sir, I do want to ask something of you that's probably inappropriate. Battalion XO already said, no medals, but I really want Stache and Specialist Yoder and Peterson to get something. It would mean so much to their families."

"What do you have in mind?"

"Bronze Star for Yoder and Army Commendation Medal for Stache and Peterson."

The general thought for a moment, then nodded. "I'll see that this happens, Lieutenant Saith."

"Thank you, sir."

The general walked through the ward and out the door.

Later, Jacob wondered what the first stupidest thing was the general had ever heard.

*

At some point in Jacob's next few early mornings, his question why God would treat people so 'badly' changed from an accusation to actually wondering. Jacob couldn't honestly say he knew much about God. 'To be fair to Doc, I should look at those chapters he wanted me to read,' he thought.

The following morning, he walked to the hospital annex where he knew there was a chaplain's office. The Specialist on duty wasn't surprised at his request for a Bible. "Of course. We have King James and RSV."

Ah. "Which do you read?"

"The RSV."

"Let me have one of those then."

Back at his cot, Jacob began reading. He read Matthew, John, Acts, and Romans in three days, then sped through all three again. Doc hadn't mentioned Matthew or Acts, but it was interesting. Whatever he expected the Bible to be, this was different. He landed on a few things that struck him forcefully—that Jesus' death was horrible and Jesus didn't want to die, but he did, making Jesus seem very real; . . . that when Paul became a believer, God already knew he was going to suffer a lot, which he did; . . . and one statement in Romans that seemed to clarify the issue for everything: if a person said to God that Jesus is Lord, and believed in his heart that God raised Jesus up from the dead, he would be saved.

'I don't understand this,' Jacob thought. 'It seems like serving God is always painful.'

'Paul, the man God chose to do great things, suffered,' Jacob thought. 'He sure got beat up a lot.' Then breathtakingly, it dawned on Jacob. 'Even Jesus suffered terribly.'

He thought. 'I don't understand why. I wonder if *anyone* understands.'

In the third week of his stay in the Nha Trang hospital, the wires were removed from his hand. The surgeon who had performed the operation was a major.

He explained what he had done. "Tendons are like rubber bands. When they're cut, they retract. So we wire the ends back together, and we do that with super-fine wire. We do a figure eight through the top tendon segment, then one loop through the bottom segment and put them together. The buttons on your fingertips hold it in place. Another wire catches the top wire and comes out your palm, so when the tendons have healed, we snip the buttons off and pull all the wires out through your palm."

Jacob cringed at the image.

"It's not as bad as it sounds."

That said, the doctor snipped the wires that held the buttons in place, then cupped his left hand into Jacob's palm to brace the finders. He picked up a regular pair of pliers, got a firm grip on the wires exiting Jacob's palm and with one strong pull, it was over. All the wires were out, and it was surprisingly painless. "Excellent, " the doctor said.

"What if the tendons had broken again?" Jacob asked.

"You'd have heard a pop," the surgeon said calmly.

He gently flexed the two repaired fingers, then instructed, "See if you can curl those fingers like you were going to make a fist. Easy now."

Jacob did so. The fingers moved very stiffly, but they moved. The doctor was satisfied. "Be gentle for about a week, then you can try to use the hand normally. Like shaking hands with someone. You won't have to baby it."

"Amazing, sir. Thank you."

The doctor looked pleased. "It *did* come out well."

Jacob paused. "Sir, can I ask you a personal question?"

The major looked a little surprised. "Ah, well, sure, I guess so."

Jacob said, "I've been wrestling with this for a long time. Do you believe in God, sir?"

The surgeon smiled and looked relieved. He held up his right hand, and looked at it. "Yes, I do. How could I not, seeing something this perfect."

That night, when Jacob woke at 4 AM, he asked God to please let him know if He was real, if He was true. 'God, I *do* want to know if You exist. Doc said somehow You could do that so it's clear, not some vague feeling.'

Jacob felt he believed in God enough now to ask. 'Please let me know, God. Please.'

The following morning, Jacob listened to the snores, and occasional groans, of the wounded men in the ward. 'Pain is sure still part of life.' He sighed. Sadly, he thought, 'Nothing's changed. It's all the same.'

But wait. It wasn't the same. Jacob suddenly found he couldn't generate the cynicism about God that had always felt so natural. He brought to mind every skeptical argument against God he could think of, but as he did so, they seemed to him as foolish, or just bitterness.

He sat up. With a growing sense of . . . what? . . . elation? . . . Jacob realized he couldn't *force* himself to disbelieve. Was this God's way of revealing Himself? Had God created belief by destroying disbelief? "I can't *not* believe," he said quietly aloud.

God had done it. And it was clear. Jacob simply couldn't make himself disbelieve in God. 'So I believe,' he thought.

He lay back down and closed his eyes. "God, I believe now." The words of the Bible came to him . . . *believe in your heart. . . believe in your heart.* It had happened. God had done it.

"I say to you, God, that Jesus is Lord, and I believe in my heart. I want to be saved."

Jacob lay still and at peace.

A little while later, a voice quietly said, "El T?"

Jacob opened his eyes. It was Billy, from LZ Polly! Jacob sat up. "Billy, what are you doing here?"

"Oh, sorry, sir, I thought you were sleeping. I'm headed home, this afternoon. My year is over," Billy said. "First Sergeant told me you were here in this hospital. I wanted to come say goodbye."

"I'm really glad you did. Wow, you get to go home today. That's great." Then Jacob asked, "Where's home, Billy?"

"Newark, Ohio. Near Columbus."

"I bet your family is so excited." Jacob paused. This was probably his one chance to find out why Stache was where he was that night. "Billy, do you have any idea why Stache was at Gun 2 the night of the attack?"

"Oh, yes, sir. Stache slept at one of the guns every night, so he could, well . . . "

"Do drugs."

"Yes, sir. He and Corporal were there that night."

41

Jacob indicated the foot of the bed. "Sit down, Billy."

"Oh, that's okay, sir. I have to leave in a few minutes. And Sergeant Tyler at Gun 1 said that after Doc had done all he could for Peterson, he started to go to Gun 2 where Stache was." Billy looked away, down the ward. "Sergeant Tyler said Doc was hit a couple of times before he got to Stache. AK 47's."

"Ah. So it was Stache who fired the beehive?"

"Yes, sir."

'And then the RPG hit the gun,' Jacob thought, 'and both men died.'

Jacob quickly changed the subject. "What about Corporal? Has anyone taken care of him?"

"Oh sir, this is great! Turns out Captain Vardman loves dogs! Corporal sleeps in the CO bunker now. He's got it made."

Jacob laughed. "That is so good! Stache would be glad." Jacob stood up. "Billy, did you know Doc Yoder re-up'ed *after* Stache got saved?"

"Yes, I did know that."

"Why?'

"Well, sir. There were two more men Doc wanted to see come to Christ. I was one of them . . ."

"And I was the other," Jacob said quietly.

"Yes, sir. I became a Christian the night of the attack." He paused, obviously wanting to hear if Jacob had believed as well.

Jacob thought, 'This may be the reason Billy came today.' He said, "Billy, I've come to believe in God and Jesus too."

Billy had a huge smile. "So it was worth it for Doc. You, me, Stache, and I think even Sergeant Tyler."

Jacob added, "And maybe a bunch of the other guys as well, in time."

"Yes, sir, I hadn't even thought about that." Billy looked at his watch. "I have to go, sir. I'm glad to have been in your unit."

"Thanks, Billy. You did well. I hope things go great for you back in Ohio!"

As Billy left, the man in the adjoining bed said. "I heard that soldier call you 'sir'. Are you an officer?"

"Yes."

"And you believe in God?"

"Yes, I guess I do," said Jacob.

"I've never heard of an officer who believed in God."

"We're not all numbskulls!"

The soldier thought this was hilarious, and laughed and laughed, until he suddenly said "Ouch!" in a loud voice, and quieted down.

Jacob put on his fatigues and walked down the ward. 'I'm a Christian now. I believe in God,' he thought. God had proved His existence by changing Jacob's heart.

The next day, sitting in the little admin office, Jacob wrote a letter of condolence to the Peterson family. Then he wrote two more letters.

> *Dear Talva family,*
>
> *My name is Lieutenant Jacob Saith. I was commanding the firebase Harold served on the night of the attack in which he so bravely gave his life in defense of the other men on the base. I cannot express how sorry I am for the loss of this good man.*
>
> *In addition to his courage, Harold's ability to maintain the critical base generators was essential for our unit to perform its mission.*
>
> *I have recommended Harold for the Army Commendation Medal for his excellence in serving his unit. You can be very proud of Harold.*
>
> *Sincerely, 1LT Jacob Saith*
> *1St Battalion / 42nd Artillery*

Jacob thought Stache's quick death at Gun 2 truly was better than the terrors of an overdose on heroin. If he'd gone back to the States, he would have faced an almost certain dishonorable discharge from the Army, and who knows what kind of short, brutal life.

The second letter was more difficult to write.

> *Dear Mrs. Yoder,*
>
> *My name is Lieutenant Jacob Saith. I was commanding the firebase your husband served on during the attack in which your husband gave his own life while helping others who had been hurt.*
>
> *I do not have the words to tell you how deeply sorry I am about the death of your husband, Jonathan. He and I had become close friends; he was one of the most caring and selfless persons I have ever known. Every man on the base held Jonathan in the highest esteem.*
>
> *I must tell you that Jonathan, or 'Doc Yoder' as we all called him, had the spiritual welfare of men on his heart, and several men on the base, including myself, came to be saved because of the truth he shared..*

He was one of the finest men I have ever met.
I have recommended that Jonathan receive the Bronze Star
Medal for his service.
Sincerely, a believer,
1LT Jacob Saith
1st Battalion / 42nd Artillery

Jacob read the letter through, then crossed out the words 'one of' and changed the word 'men' to 'man.' He put the letters in envelopes and carried them to Division HQ, where the addresses of Doc's and Stache's and Peterson's families were on file. They would address and mail the letters.

Several days later, with his travel orders in hand, Jacob boarded a Flying Tigers Airline DC-8 and headed home. He wasn't at all sure how things worked in heaven, but he hoped that Doc Yoder knew that he, Jacob, had come to believe.

The Campus

East Coast of Florida—1972

The truth will make you free.

Jesus, The Bible

THE ACADEMIC quad at 7:45, on a clear, cool Florida morning was peaceful. It was quiet except for the ubiquitous 'chut, chut, chut, sissss' sound of lawn sprinklers. The few students on the quad were headed for their eight o'clock classes, as was Jacob.

Though this was Jacob's second year as an Instructor in Humanities, it was his first fall term. He had been hired in January of the previous year, in large part, Jacob suspected, because the academic dean had served in Korea as an Army officer.

Jacob entered the classroom and noted the groggy expressions. An eight o'clock Freshman English class was definitely not one of the joys of a student's first year in college, especially on a Monday morning.

"Good morning!" Jacob said cheerfully. Nods and groans were the responses.

"Here're your papers from last Friday." Jacob quickly handed out the writing assignments from the previous week. While most students disliked writing papers, they liked getting them back to see what comments the instructor had written. Jacob worked hard to carefully read and jot notes on everyone's essays.

"Okay, it's the part I know you all look forward to—grammar!" Jacob pulled out a glass fishbowl containing slips of paper. "Today, the topic is 'find it and fix it.'" He shook the bowl. "Any volunteers?"

There were none.

"Ah, I forgot to mention the fabulous prizes for correct answers." Jacob emptied a box from his desk. "We have . . . some barely used paper clips, a rare #3 pencil, various other garbage, and the grand prize, a Snickers!"

A girl's hand shot up. "I'll go for the Snickers."

"Okay, Cass. Ambitious. But you'll have to take what you get from the bowl. #1 is a paper clip; #2 the pencil, etcetera."

Cass came up and drew out a slip. "It's the pencil. The question is, what's wrong with this sentence: 'Me and David are going to go see *What's Up Doc?*.' It should be David and I."

"Okay. Why?"

"Subjects take subjective pronouns. 'Me' is an objective pronoun."

"Good. You've definitely earned the pencil."

"But that's so easy. No one would ever say, 'Me and David.'"

Jacob nodded in agreement. "True."

And so the fish bowl grammar lesson continued. A bored looking guy won the Snickers by knowing what a gerund was. At quarter of nine, Jacob said, "Okay, for the next ten minutes, I want you to write one good paragraph on this topic: 'Who's a villain'—from movies, books, or history— and why?" Jacob wrote the topic on the greenboard. "Any villains come to mind? Anybody?"

"Hitler!"

"Norman Bates from *Psycho*."

"The banker in *It's a Wonderful Life*. What was his name . . . Potter!"

Then the student who knew what a gerund was, said, "Caroline Compson, in *The Sound and The Fury*."

Jacob was amazed. "What! You read *The Sound and The Fury*?"

"Yes."

"How'd that happen? Is it Dylan? As in Bob Dylan?"

"Well, Dylan Thomas, actually. And it was because my high school English teacher said it was the most difficult-to-understand novel ever written. So I read it."

"I agree with you about Caroline," Jacob said. "She was not a nice lady!"

Jacob looked at this watch. "Okay, one fast paragraph on a villain. And this won't be graded. I just want to see where we all are."

As the class departed, leaving their papers on Jacob's desk, Jacob asked Dylan to stay for a minute. The young man had wild reddish blonde hair, brown eyes, and granny glasses. He looked like a cross between John Lennon and a Leprechaun.

"I just wanted to say I'm impressed you read the Faulkner book," Jacob said. "And I think your teacher was right about it being difficult. How'd you do with it?"

Dylan thought a moment. "I realized the Benjy section obviously wasn't structural, but it wasn't random either. So I just read through it and enjoyed it without trying to make sense of it. It became pretty clear later on."

"Amazing. Are you going to be an English major, Dylan?"

He laughed. "No. I'd like to make a living. I just like to read. I like to read books that are challenging. I'm a math and electrical engineering major."

"Double major?"

"Yes. And I know the joke. A double major is like two different coats of paint on a car. You only see one. I like math a lot, but you can't make a living at that either, so I'll do the engineering too."

"That's going to be pretty tough academically."

Again, Dylan had the little smile. Was it a condescending smile, Jacob wondered.

"Well, Mr. Saith, I think I'll do okay."

"So what's another book you like, that challenged you?"

Dylan said, "The Uris book, *QB VII*"

"I haven't read that," Jacob said. "Thanks for the recommendation."

Jacob pointed a finger at Dylan. "Okay, quiz time. Where'd Faulkner get the title?"

Dylan said, "*MacBeth*." He squinted behind the granny glasses and quoted, "*Tomorrow and tomorrow and tomorrow, creeps in this petty pace from day to day, to the last syllable of recorded time . . .*" He paused. "I can never remember the next line."

"*And all our yesterdays have lighted fools the way to dusty death.*" Jacob added. He loved this passage.

Dylan nodded and said, "*Out, out brief candle! Life's but a walking shadow, a poor player, that struts and frets his hour upon the stage, and then is heard no more.*"

They both said the last line together. "*It is a tale told by an idiot, full of sound and fury, signifying nothing.*"

Dylan had a genuine smile now, not the bored one. "Man, that's great stuff!"

Jacob said, "Okay, question: I'm teaching American Lit next term. Do you think I could include *The Sound and The Fury*? Or is that not realistic?"

"I think it'd be great to try."

"Okay. I'll sure think about that."

As Dylan moved to the door, he stopped, and with a serious look, he said, "Please don't take offense, Mr. Saith, but I've noticed you start a lot of your sentences with the word, 'Okay.'" Then he was gone.

"Amazing," Jacob said aloud. And he wondered if Dylan really couldn't remember the line from MacBeth.

At lunch that day, in the faculty dining room, Jacob mentioned Dylan to one of the math professors. "I've got a super-smart student in Freshman English who says he's a math major."

Dr. Ackerson said immediately, "You mean Dylan Cooper. He's in my Calc 3 class. And yes, he *is* the world's smartest kid."

Jacob smiled at the superlative.

"No. I'm serious. He really is super-smart. Maybe genius."

"Isn't Calc 3 pretty advanced for a freshman?"

"Well, technically, Dylan's a junior. He got his AA in high school. And honestly, I think he's a bit bored with Calc 3."

"Did you know he's double majoring? Math and electrical engineering?"

Dr. Ackerson looked surprised. "No, I didn't. That's even more impressive."

Jacob said. "He told me he loves math, but he's doing EE so he can make a living after college."

Ackerson laughed. "Ah, a genius with common sense!"

*

Jacob seldom thought about the Army or Viet Nam, but he often thought about Doc Yoder, and their conversations. He remembered Doc speaking of people who were serious Christians. Jacob wanted very much to be a serious Christian. He intuitively knew what that implied, but he didn't know how to become one.

Since he got the teaching job at Drayton University, he'd tried out quite a few churches in the area. But the results were not encouraging.

There was the church that prohibited musical instruments. But they began each hymn with a note from a pitch pipe.

There was the church whose pastor read the announcements in a normal voice, but screamed the entire sermon at full volume.

There was the church in which Jacob, as he looked around, noticed his was the only Bible visible, and the preacher looked right at him and said, "Aha! I see we have some stuffed-shirt Baptists with us this morning!"

And there was a church that seemed pretty normal, but the sermon was frankly boring. It was mostly anecdotal stories from the pastor's life with very little reference to the Bible.

Jacob was both disheartened and surprised. He had taken for granted that churches would have the understanding and application of Bible truths that Doc Yoder had. It worried him that, from his limited exposure, this might not be the case.

One afternoon, as Jacob headed to the library, he saw a table set up near the library's main entrance. It had a sign taped to the front, 'Stump the Preacher — Win a Balloon!' Sitting behind the table was a young man with a half dozen helium balloons on long strings tied to the back of his folding chair. He caught Jacob's eye, nodded and smiled. He sure looked different than Jacob's idea of a minister. He had the big shag hair going and a mustache. He wasn't a large guy, so the big hair looked even bigger. Jacob decided he was actually pretty cool looking.

Jacob went up to the table and introduced himself. "Are you with a campus ministry?"

"Yup," the man said. "I'm Doug Cohan. The ministry's connected with a non-denominational church, Faith Chapel. Good to know one of the professors."

"Well, instructor anyway. What's the deal with stump the preacher?"

"If a student can ask me a Bible question I don't know the answer to, he gets a balloon. Or, he can skip the balloon and get a prayer said for him instead." He pointed at a small cardboard box with a slot cut in the top. "He can write out any prayer request—without a name, of course— put it in the box, and later I pray for that student."

"Interesting. Do you get many students trying to stump you?"

Doug smiled. "Actually, quite a few. The idea is just to get some conversations going. A couple of people a day ask stuff like, 'What's the fifth word in Isaiah 6,' but there're some good questions too."

"What's the last good one you got," Jacob asked.

Doug thought for a moment. "I'd say it was one a girl asked me yesterday. She wanted to know if people go right to heaven when they die, or if there's a place where they have to wait." He said, "I think there was a personal reason behind the question, but I didn't want to ask."

"What's the answer to that one?" Jacob asked.

Doug said, "Do you remember what Jesus said to the one thief who was also being crucified?"

"No, I don't. Where's that?"

"I think it's only in Luke. Jesus said to one of the thieves, 'This day you shall be with Me in Paradise!' So it sure seems like believers instantly go to be with Jesus when they die."

Jacob was impressed. "That's good. A clear answer right from the Bible." He added, "I've read Matthew, Mark and John, but not Luke yet."

"You're a Christian?"

"Yes. But I'm pretty new at being one."

"I'd like to hear how that happened." Dave said. "Maybe we could grab coffee sometime."

Jacob said, "Sure. That'd be good." Then Jacob asked, "Doesn't it get expensive buying balloons?"

Doug smiled. "Not really. Most people don't take one, even if they stump me. Maybe they don't want their friends to know they'd been talking to me, and the balloon would be a pretty obvious giveaway."

Jacob and Doug Cohan met the following day at the student union snack shop. Jacob told Doug about Doc Yoder and how God had made Himself real to Jacob.

Doug's comment was, "Thank God for people like Doc Yoder! I wish I could be more like him."

"Doc said there were Christians he called serious believers. I think he was saying they had God's view on things and trusted Him. As soon as I believed in God, I wanted to be one of those serious Christians."

"Really? I love to hear that! Do you want to get together every now and then? I can show you some things that have really helped me. "

Jacob gave this some thought. He barely knew Doug. Could this be a waste of time, or worse, getting sucked into some kind of weird ministry that might actually hurt his life as a Christian. Jacob realized he knew so little, he had no way of evaluating what was good teaching or not.

Doug said, "I know what you're thinking. You're wondering if you'll have to wear a robe and bang a tambourine in front of the library. Nope. The first guideline for growing as a Christian, is to always make sure that what people are sharing with you is right out of the Bible, and that it's clear. So you can definitely check on me if we get together. If I tell you something that's not Bible based, or doesn't seem to make plain sense, call me out on it."

Jacob laughed. "Yeah, I was wondering. But that sounds good. I'm up for it."

So Doug and Jacob met once a week, not on campus, but in a fast food place called Burger Barn, *Home of the Mushroom Burger!*

Doug talked about how he and his wife, Rhonnie, hadn't grown up in Christian homes; both come to Christ in college. "That's why we like campus ministry so much. It's a great time for telling students about Christ, and helping people grow."

"Does Rhonnie come on campus with you?"

"Sometimes, but she's got her hands pretty full with our kids. Stephen is six and Sarah's four."

They each had a mushroom burger—which were actually really good—then Doug asked a question. "Jacob, how do you know for sure you're saved, that you're going to heaven when you die?"

"Ah, well, I know I told God I believed in Him and what Jesus did. I sure feel like I'm saved."

Doug said, "Good. That conviction is really important." He made a little tripod with two fingers and a thumb. "Here's a neat way I heard to know we're saved. It's three ways the Bible says we can know. Doug wiggled his thumb. "The first way is what you just said. It's Romans 8:16, and it says, *The Spirit Himself bears witness with our spirit that we are children of God.* So the Holy Spirit of God convinces our human spirit, or heart, that we're

His children. And this is a deep conviction, not just an emotion that could change every day."

Jacob opened his Bible, the same one he'd gotten in the hospital in Nha Trang, and found the verse. He drew a little tripod in his notebook, and labeled one leg of the tripod 'Inner Conviction'—Romans 8:16

Doug picked up his index finger. "The second way is the outer evidence of our lives as we grow in our relationship with Christ. It's Galatians 5:22 and 23. *But the fruit of the Spirit of God is love, joy, peace, patience, kindness, goodness, faithfulness, gentleness, self-control . . .* I think 'fruit' here is just another way of saying the good results in a person's life as he gets closer to the Lord."

Jacob remembered Doc saying this. "The medic, Doc Yoder, said the same thing. That when he started reading his Bible and praying for his family, he became a kinder person." Jacob added, "But I didn't know what Bible verse it was." He labeled leg #2 of the tripod sketch 'outer evidence.'

Doug said, "This can take some time to become evident, but even our friends and family will notice it when it happens.

"By the way, which two of those qualities would you say you'd want more of?"

"I guess I'd say patience and self-control. I have a bit of a temper issue."

"A lot of guys pick those two."

Jacob said, "I can believe it. What's the third leg?"

"The third way we can know we're saved is the clearest one of all. God says it in black and white. It's 1 John 5:11 to 13." Doug waited for Jacob to look this up, which took a moment as Jacob was still unsure where the different books of the Bible were. When he found it, Doug quoted, "*And the witness is this, that God has given us eternal life, and this life is in His Son. He who has the Son has the life; he who does not have the Son does not have the life. These things I have written to you who believe in the name of the Son of God, that you may know that you have eternal life.*"

Jacob double underlined it in his Bible, "That's good. You're right, it's so clear. If you have the Son, you have life."

Doug put his pen in His Bible and closed it. "Yeah, it's like 'If you have my Bible, you have the pen.' If you have the Son, you have the life. The life is in the Son. No doubt or vagueness at all."

Jacob wrote next to the third leg of the tripod, 'God says it!'

"And," Doug said, "verse 13 says we can *know* that we have eternal life, not just wonder or hope."

"I like this."

Jacob suddenly realized that Doug hadn't read the verses of Scripture, but quoted them. "You knew all those verses by heart. Why'd you memorize them?"

Doug smiled. "That's a topic for another day." Then he reached over and put his hand over Jacob's notes. "So how do you know for sure you're saved?"

Jacob said, "Inner conviction, outer evidence, and God says it!" And he remembered the verses.

"Fantastic!" Doug laughed. "Next time I see you, I'm going to ask you the same question. Be prepared!"

*

A few days later, Jacob got called to the academic dean's office. This didn't worry Jacob. He and the dean, Dr. Harry Brenson, had often talked over lunch in the faculty dining room, mostly about Army experiences. Dean Brenson had been in the Engineers in Korea; indeed he still was an engineer, a PhD electrical engineer. He was relatively short, gray-haired, and powerfully built. He always seemed to have a broad smile, which belied his blunt manner. It would be an understatement to say Dean Brenson was abrupt. He communicated in bursts of brief sentences, always directly to the point with no prefaces or small talk.

When Jacob entered his office, Dean Brenson fired away. "Jacob, I have a job for you. Very short notice. Sorry about that. ECPD is here this week for engineering accreditation renewal. Dr. Habermann is under the weather. Can you do a presentation of humanities for the council?"

"Yes, sir. I guess so. When?" Jacob sometimes found himself unconsciously drawn into communicating with the same staccato rhythm as Dean Brenson. It kind of amused him, but he tried not to do it.

"Tomorrow. Eleven. In the engineering conference room." Dean Brenson stood and walked around his desk. "Very short notice. Can you do it?"

"I'll be glad to do it, Dean Brenson, but I think there must be some better qualified people in the department than me. I'm sorry to hear that Dr. Habermann is ill." Dr. Catherine Habermann was the chair of the Humanities Department.

"It's a frequent illness. And let's just say I'd like to hear your ideas on Humanities."

"I'll see you at eleven, Dean."

The Army had prepared Jacob for assignments out of the blue, and this wasn't really a very difficult one. First of all, he had nearly an entire day to prepare, and the visiting engineers would not expect, or want, Jacob to go more than 15 or 20 minutes.

At 10:55 the next morning, Jacob hauled a flip chart into the conference room, greeted Dean Brenson and the four men and two women from the Engineering Council for Professional Development.

Jacob quickly summarized the five sections of the department: English, History, Philosophy, Arts, and Psychology. He noted the number of faculty in each and the core courses presented in each. He flipped a page of the chart. The next sheet simply said, *The Philosophy of Humanities at Drayton.* There were only three bullet points under the heading.

- Humanities as stand-alone majors
- Humanities as precursors to professions
- Humanities as serving science, math, and engineering

Jacob skimmed over the stand-alone aspect, as these BA majors were well known. He mentioned that English and History were accepted by most law schools as good pre-law majors, and that psychology was a solid pre-MBA major as well as for further degree programs in clinical or research psychology.

"I think an exciting aspect of humanities," Jacob said, "is the added educational contribution they make to students who are science, engineering, or math majors. For example, there's a young man who's majoring in both math and electrical engineering who loves literature, and will certainly take our lit courses for his electives."

Jacob said, smiling, "There's even a physics professor here who can explain musical development in Beethoven like an expert. Actually, he says if you don't know math, you can't appreciate classical music. I don't know about that, but I do sense there is more of a crossover of science people who appreciate art, literature and music . . . than the other way around."

Jacob gave four more brief scenarios of humanities, such as ethics, giving cultural depth to science students. He added, "And by the way, the core humanities courses are taught in such a way that they're understandable to all majors, not just the BA students."

Jacob paused and saw both the visitors and Dean Brenson jotting notes. "So, I feel that Drayton has a really good selection of courses to serve all students, and a faculty that grasps the philosophy behind what we're doing."

Jacob glanced at his watch. Sixteen minutes. There were a few questions, but really the visiting engineers had heard what they wanted to hear. Dean Brenson gave Jacob a thumbs up, and said, "Good shot!" as Jacob left.

The unexpected follow-up of this ECPD session came a week later, when Dean Brenson asked Jacob to attend the monthly meeting of department heads. Dean Brenson told the department chairs that the ECPD had liked the presentation of how the humanities serve science and engineering. One of them said it compared favorably to an 'Ivy League school in New Jersey.' He then asked Jacob to give a quick recap of his presentation. Jacob did so, but it was an uncomfortable moment, as Dr. Habermann, was there, and she was certainly not pleased.

*

Sure enough, at Jacob's next get together with Doug Cohan, Doug asked him how he knew he was saved. Jacob drew out the tripod and paraphrased the verses.

Doug was pleased. "You'd be surprised how often Christians don't take what I call 'homework' seriously. I filled in for a Sunday school teacher once. It was a young adult class. At the end of the first class, I said, 'Read 1 Corinthians, chapter 5 for next time.'" He paused. "Guess how many in that Sunday school class had read the chapter next Sunday? None. So I closed my Bible and announced, 'The assignment for next week is the same. Read 1 Corinthians, chapter 5.' Then I left."

Doug laughed. "I heard from the pastor they were shocked. They were so used to the teacher just doing the lesson anyway, whether they'd read the chapter or not, it stunned them when I left the room."

"Why's that? I mean, why don't people take it seriously?"

"I honestly don't know. They wouldn't blow off an assignment a professor, or boss at work, gave them. Maybe it's because they know the Sunday school teacher won't check to see if they did."

He opened his Bible. "That's why I told you last week that I'd ask you the same question this time. It's kind of an accountability, I think that helps. Somebody said people may not do what we *expect*, but they'll do what we *inspect*."

He said, "Speaking of which, I have another assignment for you."

Jacob said with mock aggression, "I'll do it! I promise I'll do it! What is it?"

Doug laughed. "I'll tell you later. But right now, let me ask you a question. Who was your best friend in college?"

Jacob didn't see the point of this question, but said, "My roommate for three years, Matt Ursoni."

"How'd you guys get to be friends?"

"Well, we were around each other every day, being roommates, and we had a lot of pre-req classes together."

"So you guys talked pretty much every day?"

"Sure. About everything."

Doug said, "What I'm getting at here is that I think we can get to know God the same way you got to know your roommate. Getting together and talking and listening. I think that little times that happen a lot can be the basis of a great relationship. For example, if you and—is it Matt?—had agreed to meet once a semester for 10 hours, it's not the same as everyday for a few minutes."

"Okay, I can see that."

"And I assume that with you and Matt, it was a two-way conversation, not just him talking and you listening or vice versa."

"Right."

"Same with you and God. He speaks to us through the Bible and we speak to Him through praying."

Doug opened his Bible and read, "*And in the early morning, while it was still dark, He* (Jesus) *arose and went out and departed to a lonely place and was praying there.* Then a verse later it says His disciples found Him and said, *Everyone is looking for You.*

"I think this is so cool. Even Jesus, who was God, needed time alone to get with the Father and pray. He must have known that once the day got going, everyone was probably going to be demanding His time."

Jacob had his notebook out and was furiously writing this down. "Where was that verse you just said about Jesus going out in the morning?"

"Mark 1:35. And verse 37 is where His disciples tell Him everyone is looking for Him."

"Got it."

Doug turned to Acts. "Here's a great, great statement I love about the benefit of spending time with the Lord. It's Acts 4:13. *Now as they observed the confidence of Peter and John, and understood that they were uneducated and untrained men, they were marveling, and began to recognize them as having been with Jesus.* Peter and John had confidence—some Bibles say 'courage'— because they had been with Jesus. That's something I want big time, every day."

Jacob thought for a moment, and said, "Maybe that's why Doc Yoder was so confident. He hadn't gone to college, but he was 100 percent sure of what God wanted him to do."

"And here's an encouraging thing. It can only be a few minutes a day to have a really good relationship with God. My watch says there are 1440 minutes a day, and if I spend only one half of one percent with God, and do my normal stuff with the 99 and a half percent, it can be life-changing."

Jacob said, "Okay, I'm up for that. What's the plan?"

"Just read a short passage in the Bible, I don't know, maybe ten verses, then pray for a couple of minutes about what you read." Doug smiled. "I saw a great skit once. It was two guys at a table drinking coffee. One guy would talk about his girlfriend for a bit and the other guy would listen. Then the second guy would talk about his car problems. I mean, they were talking and listening, but on totally different topics. We Christians do that a lot with God, I think. Read His words to us in the Bible, but then pray about something totally different.

"Some people may think this is a little weird, but give it a try. Read a bit, then ask God questions about it or pray something encouraging you got."

Jacob asked, "What's a good place to start? I really like Philippians. Can I go through that again, or should it be something new?"

"Philippians would be great. And the Gospel of Luke. And Psalms. Some of them are super encouraging. In fact, let's look at Psalm 1 right now. It's only six verses long but has great stuff."

Jacob and Doug read Psalm 1 together then prayed about it. This was a little strange for Jacob, praying with someone, but it felt good too. Plus, Doug prayed in such normal language, it really seemed he was talking with the Lord. Jacob's question to God was this, 'God, what would it mean for *me* to be planted by streams of water?'

Doug said, "That was good. Are you ready for your assignment?"

Jacob said, "Yup. Fire away."

"In the second letter of Paul to Timothy, he says, *The things you have heard from me in the presence of many witnesses, these entrust to faithful men who will be able to teach others also.* See if you can find out from Scripture what the 'things' were that Timothy got from Paul. Paul meets Timothy in Acts 16, but you can look mostly at First and Second Timothy."

"Theological treasure hunt. Sounds fun,' Jacob said. "Is this for next week?"

"No. Rhonnie and the kids and I are going to spend Christmas with her family in South Carolina. So I'll be gone for three weeks. That'll give you time to do a brilliant Bible study on Paul's 'things.'"

"How many are there?"

"You tell me in three weeks!"*

As the spring term began after Christmas break, Jacob got ready for An Intro to American Lit., a course he'd been looking forward to. He didn't expect many students to sign up for the class, but was surprised and pleased when 21 students chose it as an elective. He was glad to see the name, Dylan Cooper, on the list.

The American Literature Anthology this course had used before was a good one. It was pretty inexpensive, but massive—1500 pages. It spanned poets from Frost to Ferlinghetti, and writers from Hawthorne to Poe to Vonnegut. Select passages were presented for huge works such as *Moby Dick*, but Jacob was interested to see that Vonnegut's *Sirens of Titan* was included as a complete novel. 'That's one we'll definitely discuss,' Jacob thought.

He'd decided to have them read *The Sound and The Fury*, but it meant he had to find 21 copies of the book, and pay for them himself. That he didn't mind at all. Paperback copies of Faulkner were cheap. But he was nervous about how students would react to trying to deal with this difficult novel.

At the first class, Jacob introduced himself, and wrote 'Mr. Saith—American Lit' on the board. As he turned back around, he saw that most of the guys were looking, not at him, but a girl seated near the door. And there she was. 'Oh, man,' Jacob thought, 'big time distraction.' The girl was beautiful. There was no other way to express it. Light brown hair, dark blue eyes, and stunning. She had a serious expression, but when another girl whispered something to her, she smiled, and as the Irish used to say, she smiled with her eyes.

"Okay," Jacob said, then stopped. He glanced at Dylan, a little embarrassed he'd started a sentence with 'Okay,' but Dylan didn't react. "I saw from the registration that most of you are here as an elective, not as a required English major course. So we'll approach this a little differently. We're not going to worry about how American lit developed, so we won't go chronologically. We'll jump around and read and discuss the writing that seems most interesting to us. Go through the anthology and let me know if there's something you'd really like to look at."

Jacob opened his copy of the anthology and said. "We'll begin with Edgar AllenPoe. For next time read *The Murders in the Rue Morgue*, and *The Cask of Amontillado*. For today, I'd like to get your ideas about why literature interests you. I doubt a judge assigned you this course as a punishment, like community service hours. So, what're your thoughts?"

Silence. Which was, of course, what Jacob expected. "Oh, my gosh," Jacob groaned, "maybe a judge really did make you sign up!" He smiled. "Most of the benefit of a lit class comes from discussion, so this is what I call a 'long pause' class. That is, I'll throw out a question, then wait for a long time for you all to interact. It's a bit weird if the silence goes longer than ten minutes, but that's okay. I love the tension!"

Dylan said, "I signed up because I looked at the textbook in the book store and saw some stuff I'd like to read, especially the newer writing that's edgy. Plus, I have to take an elective this term."

There were some laughs and nods of agreement. Dylan's comment got the conversation rolling, and Jacob was pleased with how the first class meeting went. It was a good precedent for future discussions.

When Doug Cohan got back from South Carolina, Jacob was prepared with a list of 'things' he'd found in Paul's letters to Timothy.

"Doug, I'm not sure I'd call these things 'things'; it seems more like what help or training Timothy got from Paul." Jacob took his list out. "Some of what I saw are inferences I made from what Paul was saying to Timothy. Here goes.

"In 1 Timothy, it appeared that Paul had taught Timothy how to instruct others, even those older than himself, and to challenge people causing problems in the ministry. Paul emphasized the need for prayer, for holy living and purity." Jacob stopped. "I think that probably means sexual purity."

Doug said, "Good. Keep going."

"In 2 Timothy, Paul points out the importance of Bible truth, and that the Bible equips people to know how to minister. He said a good minister handles the truth of the Bible accurately. I like that. Then Paul tells Timothy to share the gospel, to be an evangelist." Jacob stopped, looked at his notes, and added, "Both letters stress that Timothy should work hard at ministry. Fight the good fight!"

"Jacob, you did a great job with this! I totally agree. I'd add one more thing that's sort of implied: the benefit of having other believers around. In 2 Tim 1:16, Paul says how some hard-named guy often came and refreshed Paul in fellowship."

"A hard-named guy, huh?"

"Yup. Definitely. I don't know exactly what Paul meant by the things Timothy got from him, probably a ton we don't know. But what you found in Scripture is a very good foundation for us today. Prayer, knowing the Bible and using it to minister, sharing the gospel, fellowship and holiness are, I'd say, essential for Christians."

Jacob said, "I'm guessing there's a reason you gave me this assignment . . ."

"Yeah. I have a little deal I do on each one of those. I call them disciplines of the faith. Then there's a good Bible study on holiness, in three parts: purity, humility, and how God sees money and stuff. Are you up for all that?"

"That sounds good."

Doug said, "So, one of the last things Jesus told His followers was to make disciples of every nation. And it meant teaching these new disciples to obey what Jesus had commanded, so it was serious. I think Paul figured out the plan of how to do this. Let's go back to that verse, 2 Timothy 2:2."

Jacob found the verse and read it. "*And the things you have heard from me in the presence of many witnesses, these entrust to faithful men, who will be able to teach others also.*"

Doug said, "There's four spiritual generations in that one sentence, Paul, Timothy, faithful men, and others. That's how Paul knew disciples could be made all over the world. There's no way the relatively few mature disciples of Jesus could go to the whole world. Especially to get people to know and obey the Lord's commands."

Doug took a little booklet out of his shirt pocket. "I read the text of an amazing message a Christian leader gave years ago. His name was Dawson Trotman, and the message was called *Born To Reproduce*. It was really based, I think, on 2 Tim 2:2. The idea was that just like people reproduce physically, generation to generation, Christians can reproduce spiritually, spiritual generation to spiritual generation. The way the world got populated is how it can get the gospel shared with it."

Doug paused. "Jacob, that idea of how to do ministry has gripped me. It's compelling. It's what I want to do."

Jacob said very seriously, "Doug, I'd be glad to be your Timothy, if you think we can do that."

Doug smiled and nodded. "That's what I was hoping to hear. Thanks, Jacob. Let's do it.

"Oh, by the way, you're certainly welcome to come to church at Faith Chapel, but my senior pastor knows I don't recruit, and he's good with that. But I'd sure like it if you could come to the campus Bible study. At my house Wednesday evenings at 7 o'clock. Unless it would seem weird to you for Drayton students to know you're a Christian."

Jacob shook his head. "*Vanity, vanity, all is vanity,*" Jacob quoted for the second time ever, this time incorrectly. "If I'm that worried about being cool, I've got a big problem as a Christian!"

Doug laughed. "If we were in church, I'd yell 'Amen!' One of the things about this kind of ministry is there's no glory in it for us. Only God gets the glory. That might be a negative for some people, but it's definitely a plus for us."

Jacob reached out and shook Doug's hand. "You got yourself a Timothy."

*

Toward the end of the month, Jacob got another request, via memo, from Dean Brenson to attend the department chairs' meeting. The memo also said, 'Come see me.' Jacob had found the previous chairs meeting interesting, and was pleased to be invited again, but the puzzling situation with Dr. Habermann made it awkward.

Dean Brenson was on the phone when Jacob looked in the open door of the Dean's office. Brenson waved him in. Jacob sat down, looked around the office, and noticed a photo of a younger Harry Brenson in uniform leaning against an Army truck with barren terrain in the background. Korea, Jacob assumed. And Jacob wondered again how much he owed his job to the shared military experience with the Dean.

"Jacob, how are you doing?"

"Fine, thanks, Dean Brenson."

"Want to tell you why I've asked you to come to the department heads' meetings. Notice I said meetings, plural. I want you be Dr. Habermann's assistant."

Jacob was floored. "Dean Brenson, I don't know what to say."

"First of all, Catherine Habermann is a friend of mine. Known her for years. She's had a rough life. Husband took off. Son's worthless. Daughter, who was the good one, was killed by a drunk driver. This's all contributed to her illness. She needs an assistant to help her run Humanities. "

"I'm really sorry to hear that. But I feel so uncomfortable. Dean, I'm the new man, and the other faculty are so much better qualified. And they know it."

"Yes, they know it. That's okay. Here's an Army question. What's the difference between a hard-stripe buck sergeant and a specialist five?"

Jacob said, "The hard-stripe can command a squad. The specialist can't. Even a Spec. 7 can't command."

"That's it. Jacob, this isn't a matter of academic qualifications or tenure. They're scholars. I need a manager. Would it bother you?"

Jacob thought for a moment. This whole idea was so new. He really had no interest in college life other than teaching, but he knew he could do the task the dean was asking of him, if it helped out. Especially if it helped Dr. Habermann.

"Dean Brenson, I'll be glad to do this. But please let Dr. Habermann know that I'm *her* helper, and my role will be to serve her."

"Good shot! Let's go right now to her office, and get this change out in the open."

Which they did. The close friendship between Catherine Habermann and Dean Brenson was obvious and touching. He presented the idea of Jacob being her assistant chair in such a way that Dr. Habermann seemed both agreeable and relieved.

*

The college Bible study at Doug and Rhonnie's house was really good. They were going through the Gospel of John chapter by chapter, and Jacob was impressed by how Doug led it. He didn't really teach, but asked questions and steered the discussion that followed. The students were engaged, not just listeners.

Jacob was also impressed by Rhonnie's lively spirit and how much she enjoyed the students.

The big surprise was that the 'beautiful girl' from the American Lit class was in the Bible study. Jacob mentioned this to Rhonnie, and she said, "She is such a sweet girl! She grew up in a good church, and really seems to love the Lord. Of course, we've had to put a fence around her to keep the guys focused on the study." Rhonnie laughed joyfully. "I'll pray for her in American Lit.!"

The girl's name was Kaitlin Johansen, and in the American Lit class, Jacob was intrigued to see that as the weeks went by, Dylan Cooper managed to slowly move closer and closer to her, seat by seat. Dylan had started out sitting near the back middle of the room; he was now only two seats away from Kaitlin. Jacob thought, 'It's like watching a slow motion chase.' He wondered if Kaitlin was aware of this maneuvering, and decided, yes, she probably was.

The class had now read Vonnegut's *Sirens of Titan,* and the discussions of this dark whimsical novel were fantastic. Jacob estimated that every person in the class had spoken up once or twice to share opinions. The brilliant pessimism of Vonnegut's book resonated with college students, but interestingly, some of them felt compelled to ameliorate the book's darkness by trying to find goodness in some of the characters.

One student said she thought Salo, the inter-galactic robot messenger, was one of the kindest characters in the book. Dylan raised his hand, which no one did anymore, so it was a couple of minutes until he could speak.

"I really like Missy's comment about Salo. I think Salo is one of the most existential characters in all of literature." The room got quiet, and I think Dylan realized he'd said something that probably sounded pretentious.

Jacob tried to come to his rescue. "Interesting idea. What do you mean?"

Somewhat nervously, as though unsure how to proceed, Dylan said, "Uh, well, maybe I'm getting this wrong. So, existentialism just sees all existence as absurd, or without any meaning. It says there's no God or anything that would help people see a purpose to their lives. It seems like Vonnegut is saying that whatever causes people do the things they do, it's all random and beyond their control anyway. So once they realize that, the best thing they can do—if they decide to keep on living— is make up their own values, hopefully values that treat other people well."

"How does Salo show this," Jacob asked.

Dylan seemed to relax a bit. "We're told Salo's life purpose is to deliver a message, I guess, to the end of the universe. He didn't know what the message was. But when he found out the whole message was just a single dot, meaning 'Greetings,' the absurdity of it blew his robot mind. His whole existence was meaningless. So he committed robot suicide. He disassembled himself."

Dylan glanced quickly at Kaitlin. She was paying close attention.

Jacob, still trying to guide the discussion a bit said, "How does that make Salo existential?"

"Some existentialist, I think either Sartre or Camus, said the only important question for an existentialist is whether to commit suicide, that all other questions were secondary. Salo chose suicide. But when Constant reassembled Salo, Salo seemed to accept his new existence, and kind of redefine himself. He'd continue his mission, but now because it was his choice. And he was compassionate to Constant at the end of the book." Then Dylan added, "So I agree with Missy that Salo was kind."

"Good thoughts, Dylan." To the class, Jacob said. "Assignment for next Tuesday is 500 words on what Vonnegut's main point is in *Sirens of Titan*. Back up your viewpoint with some references from the book."

As he often did, Dylan stayed after the class to talk with Jacob. This time Kaitlin did as well.

Kaitlin's presence obviously made Dylan nervous. He said, "Thanks for bailing me out on that, Mr. Saith. That was probably ridiculous to bring the existential thing up." He seemed to be apologizing to Kaitlin, as though he were afraid she might think he was showing off.

"No, it wasn't," Kaitlin said. "I thought that was great."

The expression on Dylan's face when she said this was one of epiphany. It was as though, in an instant, Kaitlin had gone from a person who might never be a friend to a new friend who'd just praised him.

And Jacob had his own epiphany. He suddenly saw in these two a kinship. A kinship of two unusual people. She was unusually good looking, and he was unusually smart.

'She probably can't even smile at a guy without him getting interested,' Jacob thought. 'And Dylan has to be careful about sharing deep thoughts without seeming either totally out of touch with reality, or pedantic. They both have to cope with their distinctiveness.'

Even now, as they talked more about Salo and Constant from the novel, Jacob sensed in them an intuitive recognition of a shared reality. Jacob also sensed that both of them felt safe in opening up with each other. Jacob smiled inwardly. 'This is good,' he thought. 'Not beauty and the beast, but beauty and the smart guy.'

"Dylan, don't you think Salo's broken friendship with Rumfoord was part of why he killed himself?" Kaitlin asked.

Jacob thought to himself, 'He's probably thinking, 'She said my name!''

Dylan thought a few seconds, then smiled, and said, "Yeah, that's probably true. But I still think the main reason was the message he was carrying. Later, Salo called his mission a fool's errand . . . but one he was going to continue."

Kaitlin nodded, then changed topic. "I thought that was wonderful when Chrono becomes part of the bluebirds, but shouts 'Thank you, Mother and Father, for the gift of life!'"

"Me too," said Dylan. "Maybe the most positive thing in the whole story. He'd found a place to belong."

Jacob took a chance and asked a personal question. "Dylan, why'd you say it was ridiculous to bring up your idea about Salo being existential?"

"I feel like I let my guard down. I try to not—this is hard to explain— jump too far ahead of where the discussion is."

"Isn't that kind of dismissive of other people benefiting from something you'd say?"

"No, no! I don't think that at all," Dylan said quickly. He closed his eyes and gestured with his right hand, like a gentle karate chop in the air. Jacob had seen him do this in class once before when he'd brought up an obscure fact about Poe's life.

"Mr. Saith, freshman year in high school I learned something. If I said stuff in class that was interesting to me, but other people didn't get, I was just being selfish. So I came up with a plan. It's a four-step plan for going from subjective to objective."

"What do you mean?" Kaitlin asked.

"Yeah," Jacob said, "Please explain, and don't hold back even if Kaitlin and I look lost!"

Dylan laughed. "I will. This I *can* explain. So, everybody is pretty subjective. Their opinions and viewpoints are based mostly on what they feel or prefer. The trick is for people to go from their subjective viewpoint to an objective one. One that's based on facts, or the way things really are"

"What're the four steps?" Kaitlin said. "This sounds philosophical."

"It is. Let's say two people are having an argument or some kind of conflict. Step one is to be willing to consider that the other person's stance might have some validity. Step two is to try to find out as much as you can about the other person's viewpoint. Step three is to empathize—put yourself in that other person's shoes. And step four is to either modify or affirm your original viewpoint."

Dylan said, both facetiously and seriously, "Actually, this could be the answer to world peace. Just think if everyone tried to be objective about things."

"How'd that work, as far as you knowing what to say, or what not to say?" Kaitlin asked.

"I just tried to understand how other students were thinking, and why they thought that way. Then I could be myself, but considerate, so I didn't come across as a nerd or weirdo."

"I've got an example, Dylan," Jacob said. "Years ago, my father hired a contractor to redo a bathroom. The work was poorly done and took way too long. My dad was really upset and angry. How'd the four steps work here?"

Dylan said, "Ah, good. It's hypothetical, not that it didn't really happen, so I'll ask you, Mr. Saith, for guesses about the contractor. Step one: could the contractor have some valid reason for doing the kind of job he did?"

"I'll go ahead and assume yes, but go to step two."

"What did you know about the man?"

"Not much. Only two things I remember, he was always late and seemed hung over, and he always brought a thermos of milk."

Dylan asked Kaitlin, "What do you deduce from that?"

Kaitlin said, "He was an alcoholic and had an ulcer."

"Impressive! The rest we'll make up. He *did* drink too much, even on weekdays, and he had an ulcer that caused him pain. His teenage son was disrespectful, and his wife spent more than he made."

Jacob, who could actually remember the contractor, asked "How does this help?"

Dylan answered, "It doesn't change the fact that your dad probably had to hire someone else to fix the bad work, but it would let your father not be angry, or disgusted, with the man. We all have problems. Maybe your father didn't hate this guy exactly, but understanding his situation might make your dad more sad for him than mad. So your dad would be the big winner. He wouldn't have to deal with being angry with someone.

"And for me, it allows me to understand other people. So I don't think of them as unworthy, even if they do make fun of me a bit."

"Dylan, that's pretty amazing." Jacob said, and he thought, 'So this is how Dylan copes.'

Kaitlin said, "I'd add a fifth step to the plan. To have 100 percent objectivity."

Dylan looked surprised. "What's that?"

"I'm not going to tell you now," Kaitlin said. "But you should come to our Bible study. Mr. Saith comes. "

"I don't know what a Bible study is . . . " Dylan admitted.

"Then come and find out." Kaitlin said. "That's okay, isn't it, Mr. Saith?"

"Sure. I bet you'd enjoy it, Dylan."

And Dylan did start going to the college Bible study. Kaitlin introduced him as a friend from one of her classes. Doug realized, of course, that Dylan wasn't a Christian, but that made Doug especially glad he came, both for Dylan's sake and the other students who were believers. It helped young Christians avoid what Doug called the 'holy huddle,' mentality, always being around other Christians and increasingly losing touch with non-Christian friends. "Any ministry without a heart for the lost," Doug commented, "is just fellowship, not ministry."

And the next time Jacob and Doug got together, Doug said, "Let's do something a little different today. Let's go over to student apartments and just talk with people about the Lord."

Jacob's gut response to this surprised him. It was something he wanted to learn to do, because he knew telling others about Jesus was important for serious Christians to do, and he *did* want to be a serious Christian. But a bit of self-concern also came into play. There was a tiny worrisome thought. What if some of his students recognized him. His image of being a cool professor would probably suffer.

Though there were dormitories on campus at Drayton, there were several apartment complexes close by that catered to college students. The one they picked was right across from the main gate of campus, and Doug said he had already talked to the management there if it was okay for him to do a little survey with tenants. He assured the staff in the office that it was not any kind of solicitation, and they tentatively agreed to this.

Doug told Jacob there were two rules. "We don't judge and we don't preach."

The first door they knocked on was opened by two girls wearing sorority sweatshirts. Jacob didn't recognize either one.

"Hi," Doug said, "We're with one of the campus ministries and we're doing a little four-question survey. If you've got a minute, we'd love to get your thoughts." Then he added, "If you get all the questions right, you each get a million dollars."

One of the girls said, "All right!"

Doug admitted, "Well, that part's not true. We start our ministry survey with a big lie!"

The girls looked at each other, then said, "Sure, we'll do it."

"Great. Thanks! Question number one: do either of you have any church or religious background?"

"We're both Catholics,"

"Good. That's probably the biggest Christian denomination at Drayton. Did you guys know each other before you came to college?"

One girl, who seemed a bit more outgoing, said, "Since 2nd grade! We're both from Johnson High near Sarasota."

"That's cool that you got to come to the same college and room together. What're you all majoring in?"

"I'm pre-law and she's nursing."

Doug said, "I'm writing down 'super-smart' . . . with those majors."

The girls laughed but looked pleased at the compliment.

"Did you choose those because you want to help people?"

There was an interesting look exchanged between the two students. "Well," said the nursing major, "For me, it was because I thought I'd do well at it, but yeah, I guess I do want to help people. My mom is a nurse, and I really admire her for it."

The other girl said, "No one's asked me that, but honestly, I don't know. I know I love lawyer shows on TV. I'm not really sure if I'll do law school."

"Second question: on a scale of one to ten, what number would you give your own interest in spiritual, or even philosophical, things? I don't mean, how often do you go to church, or even if you go at all, but just kind of the you and God connection?"

Pre-law said, "Probably a five."

Nursing said, "A nine, definitely."

The first girl looked at her friend with an astonished expression. "Really, Karen? A nine!?"

"Yeah. I think about that stuff a lot." She smiled. "I even pray sometimes."

Doug told Jacob later that this wasn't unusual, for even long-time friends to not be aware of each other's religious interests.

"Okay, the third question is this: if you could change anything about religion, either from your own experience, or a big world-wide sense, what would it be?"

"Well, we both went to the same church back home, so we'll probably agree on this one. Our church sure seems to talk about giving a lot, a whole lot. I mean giving to the church."

The nursing student said, "I'd say the church can be kind of judgmental about stuff, like what clothes you wear to church. But we have a young priest for the new assistant pastor, and he's pretty cool. It's probably just the older people not liking what young people do. Oh! That's another thing I'd change. Make the mass more toward young people."

Doug was writing down their answers quickly on his survey pad, "Those are great answers.

"Here's the last question, and it's the toughest. How would you define what a Christian is?"

There was quite a pause as the students considered this. Pre-law said "Obviously, someone who believes in God, and treats other people how they want to be treated."

"The golden rule," the other said. "And someone who doesn't judge others."

"Hey, good thoughts! Wouldn't it be great if everybody did those things?"

Doug turned the pad of survey forms over and drew on the back of one. "Here's another way to look at that." It was a simple sketch of two 'cliffs' separated by a gap. He drew a stick figure of a person on one cliff, and the word, 'God' on the other. He said, "I won't try to draw a picture of God, so

I'll just write 'God' here. There's some neat statements in the Bible about what a Christian is." He paused. "Do either of you have a Bible handy?"

"I do," said the nursing student. She walked away to get it. While she was gone, Doug asked about the girl's sorority. "I haven't heard of that one."

"It's pretty new, just gone national. It's been at Drayton for three years now. Karen and I are juniors, but we're just pledging."

"That's great. Hope that's a good experience for you. I'm Doug, by the way, and this is Jacob."

"I'm Laurel."

The other girl returned with her Bible, which was white with gold edging on the pages.

Doug smiled and said, "See if you can find a chapter called Romans. It's about four fifths toward the end." He watched as she opened the Bible to the book of Acts. Tiny flecks of gold paint popped off the edges of the pages. "Just a handful more to the right. The next chapter is Romans. Find a big number 3, and the 23rd statement . . . little number 23."

"You want me to read that?"

"Yeah, please."

Karen read, *"For all have sinned, and come short of the glory of God."* She added, "I think this is kind of an old-fashioned Bible." She looked at the cover. "It says *King James.*"

"No, that's good. 'Sin' is a sort of a religious term. How would you explain what sin is to one of your friends who didn't grow up in church?"

Laurel said, "I guess just doing wrong things?"

"Yeah," Doug said. "Exactly. And it says that everyone does this. Do you guys agree with that, that everybody does wrong stuff?"

"Sure. Not murder or robbing banks, but something."

"So on my little picture, I have two cliffs, and a space between people and God. It just means people are separated from God. It's because if I sin and God is holy and pure, and I went to Him the way I am, I'd pollute Him. It's not that God is a snob, but it's like if you're doing a chemistry experiment with distilled water, and someone throws dirt in it, the experiment is ruined."

The girls seemed to agree. This was probably something they'd heard in church before.

Doug said, "Now go back maybe fifty pages, to a chapter called John. See if you can find John, section 3, and statement number 16."

Karen turned pages quickly. "Got it."

"Wow, you're good at that!"

Karen read, "*For God so loved the world, that He gave His only begotten Son, that whosoever believeth in him should not perish, but have everlasting life.*"

Doug asked, "Does that sound familiar?"

Laurel said, "No, I don't think so."

Doug didn't ask a question about this verse, but just stated, "This says that God really loves people, even while we're doing wrong things, and makes a way for people to get with Him. It's through the Son." Doug smiled. "You both know this stuff, I'm sure, being Catholics." He paused. "So the question is, what did Jesus do that if people believe it, they have everlasting life?"

Karen said, with a very serious expression, "He died on the Cross." There was a definite capital 'C' to her word, Cross. Jacob wondered if she saw this as wonderful, or as a gruesome reality of her church upbringing.

"Yes. But how does that let people be with God?"

Neither girl answered.

"Just two more fast statements. Karen, see if you can find a tiny chapter called 1 Peter. It's past Hebrews, almost to the end of the Bible. It's section 3, and statement 18."

Karen found it and read, "*For Christ also hath once suffered for sins, the just for the unjust, that he might bring us to God, being put to death in the flesh, but quickened by the Spirit.*"

"So what do you think that one is saying? The word 'quickened' just means brought back to life."

Laurel said, "Like Karen mentioned, Jesus died. Is this saying this is how Jesus brings us to God? It says, the just for the unjust. So I guess Jesus dies instead of us?"

"Laurel, that's one hundred percent right. Exactly! That's the whole deal of the Christian faith. We do the bad things, but Jesus pays for it. It's what Jesus does that brings us to God.

"It's like if you had a four-year-old niece who broke something in a store. She's four and can't pay for it, but you care about her and take out your credit card and pay for the damage. She did it, but can't pay for it. You didn't do it, but can pay for it. Somebody said, 'Jesus pays a debt He doesn't owe, because we owe a debt we can't pay.'"

Doug drew a bridge, in the shape of a cross lying on its side, across the gap between the two cliffs. "This is the way people can get to God, by crossing the bridge Jesus has built."

He paused. "Do you think this means everyone is going to heaven?"

"I don't know," admitted Laurel.

"One last statement. Karen, you are so fast at finding these. I'm amazed. Last chapter of the Bible, Revelation, section three, and the 20th statement."

Again, Karen found this verse quickly. "*Behold, I stand at the door, and knock; if any man hear my voice and open the door, I will come in to him, and will sup with him, and he with me.*" Karen said, "I think our church has a picture of this in the chapel. Jesus knocking on a door."

"I've seen a picture like that too." Doug said. Then he asked. "What's the door Jesus is knocking on, do you think?"

"The door to heaven?" Laurel said.

"Good. Karen, any thoughts?"

"To our souls?"

"Those are really good answers," Doug said. "You're right. It's Jesus knocking on the door of a person's life. The doorknob is on the person's side, because God doesn't force Himself on anyone. It's each person's choice whether she wants to be with God by opening the door of her life.

"But it's cool that Jesus says if a person does open the door, He says He will come in and fellowship with her. Great way to think of being a Christian, having that kind of relationship."

Karen reached out and took the sketch. "Can we keep this?"

"Sure. If I win the Nobel prize, it'll be worth at least a dollar." Then Doug said,

"Can I be a bit pushy, and ask you guys where you'd put yourself on this little picture?"

They both looked at the sketch. Laurel finally said, "Probably somewhere in the middle of the bridge."

Karen nodded agreement. "Me too."

Doug said gently, "Yes, I know what you mean. But here's the great thing: all it takes is just saying to God, 'I want to be with You, and I open the door of my life. I know Jesus died for my wrongs, and I'm glad for that.'

"This is just between you and God, in private. And when a person does this, she has everlasting life, and knows she's going to heaven."

Both girls were silent, looking at the picture of the cliffs and the bridge. Jacob wondered what was in their minds when they said they were in the middle.

"Thanks so much for doing our little survey! You both are super intelligent. I hope your studies go well."

Both Karen and Laurel thanked us for coming. They closed their apartment door, and as we left, we heard faint sounds of them talking.

"Doug," Jacob said, "That was incredible! I had no idea you could do something like that . . . that they'd talk with us and let you share with them. They even thanked us!"

Doug just smiled. "Let's see if we can talk with one more person, then we'll quit."

We knocked on two more doors. One said he was studying for a test, and the second did the survey, and said he was Jewish. Doug said, "Great," and did a variation of the same illustration, but with Old Testament verses about the Messiah that conveyed the same concepts as the New Testament statements. Jacob was impressed how natural and versatile Doug was in connecting with people. The girls and the Jewish student were quite different, but Doug related easily with them.

Jacob and Doug talked at length after leaving the apartments. Jacob was fired up and excited about what he'd just seen.

Back at the Burger Barn, Doug gave a quick explanation for why he interacted with students the way he did. "With college students, I keep the conversation pretty light-hearted. That's why the silly comment about the million dollars. If I'm tense or serious, they'll be tense. But if I'm relaxed, they relax. I wouldn't do this same approach though if I were talking to older people in a neighborhood. Then it's polite deference.

"Also, I look for ways to give some words of praise."

"Yeah, I noticed that. I thought that was good. The girls seemed pleased."

"It lets people we're talking with feel like we're on their side. That's what I meant when I said we don't ever preach at or judge people."

Jacob said, "I wondered why you said those were great answers when the girls said what they thought a Christian was."

Doug nodded. "Our goal at student apartments is simple, to show that little gospel illustration. A verse in Isaiah 55 says when God's word goes out—and when *we* share, it's going out—it doesn't come back empty. It has the effect on people that God intends. Like my shop teacher once said, 'Let the tool do the work.'

"Of course, if this were in Bible study, and somebody said something wrong, like all religions lead to God, we'd definitely correct that." He added, "In a polite but clear way, so no one would be confused."

"I liked your illustration. And that you drew it out."

"Thanks! It's called the Bridge. I'm not sure who came up with it. What I do is my own version of it. I call it SDSD, All 3"

"What'd you mean?"

"The first verse is S . . . people's situation—separated because of sin. Then it's D . . . meaning God's desire, for people to have eternal life.

The second S . . . is God's solution, Jesus pays for their sin so they can go to God. And the last is D . . .peoples' decision."

Jacob said, "And each verse is from a Chapter 3! I like it. That's pretty easy to remember."

Doug leaned forward. "Can you remember it right now?"

Jacob could. He couldn't quote the verses, but he could easily remember the order of them, and basically what each verse said.

"You've got a good memory. Next time we go out, you can ask the survey questions, and I'll do the Bridge. Then whenever you want to, you can do the whole deal."

"Do churches and other groups do this too?" Jacob asked.

"Some do probably. Not at Drayton that I know of. Some Christians think that who gets saved is pre-determined, and that sharing the gospel like this is unnecessary."

Doug frowned. "If that's actually true, I'll have to apologize to the Lord when I get to heaven. But until then, I go with Paul who said, 'Woe is me if I don't preach the gospel.' Paul was an idiot if what he did was meaningless, because he sure got treated badly for doing it."

"So why would Christians not tell people about Christ? I mean, aside from the pre-determined thing?" Jacob asked.

"Jacob, that's probably the question for the centuries! Let me tell you why *I* do it anyway, then I'll give you my thoughts on why people might not."

"Okay."

"I do this, " Doug said, "because when I read Revelation 20, it says anyone whose name isn't written in the book of life is thrown into the lake of fire. Jacob, I think that's literally true. And Romans 10 says anyone who calls on the name of the Lord will be saved, but they can't call on the Lord if they've never heard of Him. Someone has to tell them. I want to be a person who tells people about Christ so they can at least make a decision."

Jacob said, "I do too, Doug. That was really good today!"

"Ah, and here's my favorite verse: in Acts 4, the disciples were told by the authorities in Jerusalem not to speak about Jesus to anyone. Here's the part I love. Peter says, 'We cannot stop speaking of what we have seen and heard.' Isn't that great? They *couldn't not* tell people about Jesus! So their 'discomfort zone,' if that's a word, was not *telling* people, but *in not telling* people. That's how I want to be."

"Seems to me that's how you are . . . "

Doug shook his head. "No, not yet. I still chicken out sometimes."

"So back to the question. What's your idea on why Christians don't do this?"

"There are probably several, some understandable. Like a person not feeling they know enough, or that since they still sin, they're not good enough to tell others about the Lord.

"But I think the big reason is embarrassment."

"Really? People are embarrassed about being Christians?"

"Not of *being* Christian, so much, but of identifying that way to their non-Christian friends or co-workers. You can say 'God' all you want, and no one gets too upset. But say 'Jesus Christ,' and it's different. Anyway, Paul said 'I'm not ashamed of the gospel; it's the power of God for salvation.' He didn't say 'I'm not *afraid* of sharing the gospel,' but not *ashamed*. And Jesus even said if anyone was ashamed of Him or His word, He'd be ashamed of him before God. That's strong."

"Wow. Where's Jesus say that?

"In Luke 9:26

"Anyway," Doug continued, "That's my thoughts. I think I'm a little like Timothy. I'm kinda timid at times, but I want to obey Scripture and do the work of an evangelist. And maybe it'll mean, somehow, that someone won't end up in the lake of fire because of it."

"I've never heard it like that before. I know Doc Yoder was committed to it, and now I think I know why. Will you train me in this?"

"Of course. I'm glad to have someone to go out with me. This will be great."

*

As the Spring term came to an end, Jacob was encouraged that the decision to add *The Sound and The Fury* to the American Lit course was moderately successful. It was encouraging in that most of the students made a good effort to read the book, and, with Dylan's help, to make sense of it. Dylan had repeated his earlier comment that it was the most-difficult-to-understand novel ever written. Perhaps that gave a kind of elite status to it, and made the struggle to read it seem worthwhile. Jacob doubted if many of them had finished the book, but he was proud of them for trying.

Jacob was also encouraged that his relationship with Dr. Habermann had become cordial, even friendly. They both attended the department chair meetings, and Jacob had made it clear to the other department heads that he was a lowly assistant, not an unqualified intruder. He also won approval by volunteering to take notes of the meetings, a task everyone else hated. At the last meeting for the term, Dean Brenson mentioned in passing that he had put Jacob on a twelve-month contract. This was a mixed blessing, as it meant Jacob wouldn't have summers off, but it also meant an increase in salary. The most positive aspect of this promotion, to Jacob, was it demonstrated the Dean's confidence in him.

It took a little longer for Jacob to gain the same degree of approval from the faculty of the Humanities Department. There were no objections vocalized, but a decided coolness prevailed at staff meetings. However, the disgruntled feelings faded as Jacob took on a lot of menial chores, such as conflict resolution at registration and arranging for proctors at final exam time. Doug had once mentioned to Jacob that the greatest eliminator of resentment was humility. This certainly seemed to hold true for people's acceptance of Jacob's new role at the university.

Doug's Bible study in the Gospel of John continued into the summer, though with fewer students. Jacob was profoundly impressed with one statement of Jesus in chapter 17. He basically said that the same reason the Father had sent Him into the world, He was now sending the disciples into the world. It was like a transfer of a job description. Jacob was again struck with the realization that being a serious Christian meant a deep commitment. It was awe-inspiring for Jacob to think of himself doing a ministry as the Lord had done it, but—as with the Lord—it would not be easy.

Kaitlin was staying for the summer term. As an elementary education major, she had a required teaching internship. She would be an unpaid teacher's assistant and 'shadow' for a remedial class in a public school. Not surprisingly, Dylan also decided to stay for the summer.

Dylan said very little during the Bible studies. When he did speak, he seemed, uncharacteristically for Dylan, unsure of himself. He appeared to wrestle with understanding the gist of the Bible passage, but Doug always thanked him for his comments.

After one Bible study, Jacob mentioned this to Doug. Doug showed him a passage of Scripture in 1 Corinthians 2 that stated that a non-Christian can have a difficult time trying to understand spiritual principles because Bible truths are 'spiritually appraised.'

Doug said, "This is a generalization, and obviously, a non-Christian who is sincerely looking for truth in the Bible can find it. Like you did with your grasp of the importance of Romans 10:9, the 'believe it in your heart' verse.

"It probably sounds a bit judgmental, but what people say in Bible studies usually lets me know where they are spiritually."

Dylan hung around at the end of one Bible study. There was something obviously bothering him. He said to both Jacob and Doug, "I asked Kaitlin if I could take her to dinner, and she said she couldn't do that. That she couldn't have a date with someone who wasn't a believer. Is that true?"

"Oh, Dylan, I'm sorry," Doug said. "Yeah, it kind of is."

"Did I just hurt my friendship with her by asking her out?"

"No, no. Definitely not! Is that what you were worried about?" Dylan nodded. "Yeah. I mean, it took me a week to get the courage to ask, but then she seemed so sad, I was sure I'd messed things up." He added quietly. "I've never dated anyone before."

"She's still your friend, Dylan. You can be sure of that."

Jacob thought, 'He likes her. But he's anxious. He's afraid he could lose this wonderful friendship.' Jacob also realized that Kaitlin also probably liked Dylan, possibly a rare relationship for her, guarded as she must have to be, and that she might also be sad about maybe losing Dylan as a friend.

Doug and Jacob continued to go to student apartments twice a week. Doug had gradually transferred over to Jacob the little gospel interaction, step by step. Now, after four or five weeks, Jacob was doing the whole thing, start to finish. Jacob thought this was a great way to train someone in something a person might find a little scary.

Doug told him that when he asked anyone to come with him to share with students, he said that the person didn't have to do a thing, or say anything, that Doug would do it all. "Just come be with me," was how Doug put it. "Jesus kind of did the same thing in John 2. He took the disciples up to Jerusalem and threw out the Temple merchants. The disciples were just with Him, watching this happen." Doug laughed. "That must have blown their minds. They were probably in awe of the Temple and its splendor, and here's the guy they're with tearing the place up. I love it!"

During the summer weeks, Doug led Jacob through what he called 'follow-up plans,': how to do Bible study, how to *lead* a good Bible study, effective prayer, fellowship, and the three character areas they had briefly discussed before. Jacob felt he was getting the solid foundation of a relationship with God he had wanted so much. His delight was doing Bible study on his own. To Jacob, the Scripture was so clear, so compelling. And he felt, more and more, that it was a privilege to serve God. He prayed for God to give him a man he could help in the same way Doug was helping him. He thanked God over and over for allowing him to meet Doug.

Three weeks following the conversation with Dylan about asking Kaitlin out, something wonderful happened. The Bible study group was discussing the nineteenth chapter of John, and Dylan spoke up. This time there was no uncertainty in his voice.

Dylan said, "When I read verse 28, that Jesus knew that all things had been accomplished, I remembered a couple of other verses where Jesus *knew* something. In chapter 13, when He washes the disciples' feet, it said He knew that He'd come from God and was going back to God. Then in 17:4, it says Jesus knew He'd accomplished the work the Father sent Him to do. Since He hadn't died yet, this must mean preparing the disciples for ministry. So Jesus knew He was going back to heaven, He knew He'd accomplished the work of training the disciples, and He knew that His death accomplished all that was needed for peoples' salvation."

Someone who was furiously taking notes, asked, "Dylan, what are those verses again?"

"Thirteen three, seventeen four, and twenty, verse 28."

"Thanks. That's really good."

Dylan closed his Bible, and commented, "It seems like we can know those same things: security because we're going to God; that we can train others to serve, and what Jesus did on the cross accomplishes everything."

Jacob thought, in amazement, "That's unbelievable! What an insight. From Dylan!"

He glanced over at Doug. Doug looked like he was going to cry. Doug nodded slowly. Dylan had come to Christ.

After the study concluded, Dylan quickly left, but Kaitlin stayed. She had an intense look on her face. "Is Dylan a Christian now?" she asked Doug and Jacob.

"From what he shared in the study tonight," Doug said, "I'd say yes. I was so surprised and happy. Has he said anything to you, Kaitlin?"

"No. And I know why he hasn't. He's afraid I'll wonder if he's done it to impress me." She looked sad. "Which is wrong. He ought to realize I know his character better than that."

Jacob said, "I think he *was* worried about that, Kaitlin. But I agree with you. Dylan has integrity. He wouldn't fake this."

"This is so confusing. What should I do?"

Doug smiled. "Talk to him. Let him know." Doug laughed. "Anyway, he kind of gave himself away tonight!" Then Doug added, "Jacob, would you get with Dylan and show him some of the stuff we've been doing?"

Jacob said, "Definitely. I'd love to do that."

So Jacob began to meet with Dylan every week. Not surprisingly, Dylan easily absorbed all that Jacob presented. He immediately asked if he could go out with Jacob to the student apartments to share the gospel. Jacob was nervous the first time they went. It was Jacob's first time without Doug, and Jacob prayed silently, 'God, *please* let this go well. Don't let it be discouraging for Dylan.'

Whenever Doug and Jacob went to apartments, they prayed in advance that God would lead them to students who were ready to listen. Or, as Doug once prayed, "Lord, lead us to the people you want us to meet, no matter how they respond. Whether they're friendly or hostile. Thy will be done!"

Jacob prayed this with Dylan, and God gave them an exciting, fruitful time. They met four students in one apartment, two guys and two girls. They agreed to take the little survey, Jacob suspected, in order to give him and Dylan a hard time, but the atmosphere got relaxed very quickly. Dylan shared a little of how he came to believe in Jesus, and Jacob showed the students the Bridge illustration. All four listened carefully, and answered Jacob's questions without sarcasm. One of the guys asked if he could keep the illustration. Jacob was impressed how often this happened, that someone asked to keep the sketch.

The exciting time was an answer of God to Jacob's prayer. Dylan was silent as they walked back to campus. Finally he said, "Did you see how things changed when they heard the Bible?"

'Ah, I can tell him Isaiah 55:11,' Jacob thought. "Dylan, Doug gave me a great verse for what happens when God's word goes out." Jacob quoted the verse. "It's an assurance for us that no matter what happens, God uses it in a person's life. Even if they seem to reject it, it's doing what God wants."

Doug had cautioned Jacob that though Dylan was like a skyrocket right now, there could be discouragement down the road, as Dylan grew in his faith. "There're a lot of ups and downs in the early months,"

But Jacob thanked God every day for the chance to meet with Dylan and see him become more and more solid in his faith.

*

Toward the end of summer term, a problem arose. A student had made a complaint about Jacob being at the student apartments with a Christian ministry. Jacob learned of this from Dean Brenson.

"Jacob, you did tell me you were a Christian when you came on board. That's fine with me. As you probably know, my wife, Marilyn, goes to church. Didn't know you were doing some ministry here at Drayton though."

"Dean, can I ask what the complaint was?"

"Andy Stevens brought it to my attention."

Jacob knew Dr. Stevens was the chair of Biology.

"Andy said a bio major told him, quote, 'Mr. Saith was preaching at the apartments.' Student said he thought you favored Christians in your classes. Said he got a bad grade in your Freshman English class."

"Dean Brenson, it's true that I'm part of a campus ministry, and I do go to one of the student apartments to talk to students. As far as a bad grade, no one really gets a bad grade in Freshman English! Unless they just don't show up for class."

Jacob was upset. Harry Brenson was a fair man, and Jacob could tell he wasn't angry with Jacob. But he was perhaps disappointed that he'd been put in an uncomfortable position. Jacob had once tried to share with Dean Brenson, very respectfully. But the Dean had simply commented, "I understand people being religious. But I'm a scientist, so I can't believe."

Now Dean Brenson said, "Of course, I'm not going to tell you, you can't practice your religion. Won't do that. But it *can* have the appearance of partiality. That's never good. Let's both think about this and come up with a solution."

"Yes, sir." Jacob said. "Thank you."

Jacob told Doug about the student's complaint the next day. Doug was surprised and saddened. "Jacob, I'm so sorry. This puts you in a tough spot. Romans says we're to obey civil authority, and even though your boss didn't say you can't, he obviously wishes you'd stop going to apartments."

"Sure. But I can't stop sharing the gospel, no matter what anyone wishes, or even forbids . . . "

"True."

"What do you think? Is there a solution to this?"

Doug looked out at the parking lot, where several Drayton students were leaning against a car, talking and laughing. He turned back to Jacob with a determined expression. "Well, one short-term solution is for you and Dylan to go to some of the neighborhoods around the church instead of student apartments. My pastor would sure love that. Older people need to hear the good news too."

"Is that as good as student apartments?"

"Well, no. Not really. There's usually a bit more resistance." Doug appeared to be struggling with some idea or thought, as though he wasn't ready to share it. "Ah, well, let me just say this straight out. Rhonnie and I are probably going to move up to the Orlando area next year. I've been asked by my denomination to be the associate pastor of a church there." Again, the long pause. "Would you consider coming with us?"

"What? Really?"

"Yeah, I know this is pretty radical. And I'm not trying to persuade you. This is just me thinking out loud. It's an invitation, not recruitment."

Jacob didn't say anything for several moments. Then he asked, "Okay. Tell me your thoughts on this."

"Jacob, you're comfortable on a campus. You connect with college students. Kaitlin and Dylan even said the way you teach classes is like how we try to get Bible study leaders to do it." Doug shook his head. "It just seems if you couldn't do campus ministry, and that means evangelism too—it would be a shame. If Drayton has a problem with a professor doing this, it might be good for you to think about going into full-time ministry on a campus somewhere. Like Orlando. There's a campus up there."

"Doug, It's hard to picture right now. Let me think about this."

"Of course. It kind of surprised me too that I even mentioned it. And part of it is selfish. I'd sure like to get more time with you in ministry."

At lunch in the faculty dining room a few days later, Dean Brenson sat down next to Jacob. The Dean looked around the room. There were only a few people having lunch, so it was easy to talk. "Have you thought more about our little situation, Jacob?"

"Dr. Brenson, I'd be happy to talk with people about God in the neighborhoods around my church, rather than the student apartments. That way, there's no connection with the school."

The dean looked pleased. "Ah, good. That seems like an excellent solution." He thought for a few seconds. "Jacob, I'm sorry about all this. Andy Stevens said you're probably right about the kid getting a bad grade. He's not a good student."

"No sir. I'm sorry I put you in an awkward spot."

"Here's the deal. I've talked with Catherine. She appreciates how you've stepped in to help with the department. It was *her* suggestion to make you the chair for this coming year. She said she'd be glad to retire. It's what I want, but I didn't bring it up. She did."

For the second time in a few days, Jacob was caught off guard. "Dr. Brenson, I'm kind of stunned. Thank you. It's an honor to even be considered for this."

Dean Brenson said, "It is unusual. But I think it will work well. Oh, and you'd have to begin work on your PhD. Don't say anything right now. Let's meet in a week. You give me your decision then."

"Yes, sir. I will. Again, thank you."

Jacob didn't mention the dean's offer to Doug when they met at Burger Barn, to avoid any sense of competitive confusion. They talked about what it would look like if Jacob decided to join Doug and Rhonnie in Orlando. The college, FTU, Florida Technological University, was small, but gaining in size every year.

"Jacob, this is not an easy job. There's an old hymn, *So Send I You*, that some Christians think is absurdly extreme. It says 'So send I you to labor unrewarded, to serve unpaid, unloved, unsought, unknown . . . '" Doug smiled. "Yeah, not a job description you'd see in a want ad. But pretty realistic for this kind of ministry."

Doug made it clear that the 'unpaid' lyric of the song was appropriate. Jacob would have to support himself financially. The church had no budget for a full-time campus minister.

Jacob said, "That's no big deal. I have money enough from the Army to live for two years, and I could get part time jobs." And he added, "If I think this is what God wants me to do."

"We both need to pray about this big time. You know that verse in John 8 where it says the truth will make you free?" Doug leaned forward, which Jacob had come to see as Doug being very serious.

"A person has to be free in some important areas. Ministry can be so hard and discouraging, that if a person's commitment isn't a hundred percent, that person will probably give up."

"What're the areas?"

"We need to be free from fear, from worry about money, from doubting God no matter what happens, and from lust and loneliness. Ministry can be very lonely at times."

Jacob wrote this down. "What are the Scriptures on those?"

Doug said, "*You* do a study on those. Then pick just one key verse on each one. Ask God to give you those verses as life verses. When discouragement hits, and it will, you've got those Scriptures like stakes driven into the side of a mountain."

"I'll do that." Jacob said. "I'll let you know."

The following four days marked the turning point in Jacob's life. His summer classes were on a Tuesday / Thursday schedule, so he had Friday through Monday to think about his decision. There was an abandoned WWII airport in nearby Valkaria, and Jacob drove there each morning to study and pray. It was pleasant to walk the old runways for an extended time of prayer.

After two days of study, Jacob chose four 'freedom verses' and asked God to make these his stakes anchored in the mountain.

To combat fearfulness, Jacob memorized Romans 8:15. *For you have not received a spirit of slavery leading to fear again, but you have received a spirit of adoption as sons by which we cry out, 'Abba! Father!'* Jacob remembered Doc Yoder's comment about God delivering him from fear after his mother's death. And Jacob thought, 'I'm a child of God now. He'll guard me.'

Not worrying about money seemed easy to Jacob; his father was a good provider, and Jacob intuitively transferred this assurance over to his heavenly Father. The verse he chose was Hebrews 13:5 . . . *being content with what you have, for He Himself has said, 'I will never desert you, nor will I ever forsake you.'*

. . . *taking every thought captive to obedience to Christ* . . . was Jacob's preventative Scripture to fight the lifelong battle for sexual purity. Jacob recognized lust began in the thought life, so fighting the battle at this early stage helped preempt thoughts that led to sin.

Perhaps the most difficult was to find a life verse that would combat doubt. He considered Romans 8:28, that all things work together for good, the verse Doug sarcastically said every Christian knew and no one believed. But Jacob finally decided that Colossians 1:16,17 would be his life verses to give him peace of mind that God was sovereign—wise, loving, and powerful— no matter what happened. . . . *all things have been created by Him and for Him. And He is before all things, and in Him all things hold together.*

'In Jesus, all things hold together,' Jacob reflected. 'Jesus is the glue of the universe, that holds everything together.' Jacob thought. 'If Jesus ceased to exist for even a second, the universe would disappear. That's probably bad theology, but that's how I'm going to think of it.'

The final verse of Scripture Jacob prayed about was Galatians 5:1, because it was the ultimate 'freedom' verse. Jacob memorized it, and quoted it to himself as he walked. *It was for freedom that Christ set us free; therefore, keep standing firm and do not be subject again to a yoke of slavery.* Jacob knew that this admonition was aimed at Jewish Christians who tended to revert back to the Jewish Law, but Jacob asked himself if there were anything from his life before Christ that he'd a tendency to fall back on.

This led him to two realizations: that he honestly couldn't think of anything he valued from his past that represented a threat to his serving God wholeheartedly, and that he couldn't think of a life verse to combat loneliness, because it didn't seem relevant. He had never been lonely. While someone had once told him that loneliness was the worst feeling a human could experience, he had never felt it.

Jacob knew he'd choose to go with Doug and Rhonnie to Orlando. He certainly loved teaching college classes, but he recognized that he was a person who couldn't do two things at once. He couldn't be effective in ministry *and* the academic life. He was sure there were certainly many people who could do both, but he could not. He realized, 'I'd be a good professor or a good minister, but not both.'

And the implication of Doug's statement months ago, that the goal of his life was to keep as many people as possible out of the lake of fire, was compelling. Jacob now saw his life in the same light.

The decision was made.

On the following Wednesday, Jacob met with Dean Brenson to tell him the decision. Jacob told him that he was the best boss he'd had ever had, being both supportive and challenging, but that he'd decided to go into Christian ministry.

Interestingly, the dean seemed to have anticipated this outcome. "I figured that was going to be your choice. Don't know why I thought that. I mentioned it to Marilyn, and she said, 'Of course that's what he's going to do.'"

"Dean, if it's okay with you, I'll stay on and teach this coming Fall term. Hopefully, that'll give enough time for another person to help Dr. Habermann. I do feel badly about disappointing her."

Dean Brenson stood up and extended his hand to Jacob. "Can't say I totally understand your decision, but you've done a good job here. I'll give you a letter of recommendation. Might come in handy sometime."

"Thank you, Dean. I appreciate everything you've done to help me."

Doug's response was both pleased and a little apprehensive. "I've never asked someone to give up so much before." He was perhaps nervous that he'd gotten Jacob into something Jacob might later regret.

Jacob shook his head. "Actually, I'm glad to have great job I can give up. If I'd had a job I hated, it wouldn't be the same. This is good!"

At one of the last Bible studies of the summer term, Jacob saw Dylan and Kaitlin talking together. They were laughing about something. Rhonnie Cohan said to Jacob, in her Southern vernacular, "Aren't they just the cutest little things you've ever seen!"

Jacob had told Dylan about the plan for the coming year, that Jacob would be here at Drayton for the Fall term. He asked Dylan if he minded going to neighborhoods near the church instead of student apartments. Dylan knew about the complaint lodged against Jacob for 'preaching' at apartments.

"Of course. It'll be interesting to see the difference." Then he added, "But if it's okay with you, I'd still like to go to the apartments. You know Brett from Bible study? He wants to come with me. Do you think I'm ready to train someone else?"

"Yes! You sure are! That's fantastic about Brett. Show him some of the other things we've been going through."

"I'd like to keep the Bible study going too, after you and Doug are gone. Can you show me how to lead it?"

Jacob had prayed this very prayer for the past week, that God would put on Dylan's heart to continue with the ministry. It was scary because he was such a young believer, but Jacob felt he could do it without falling into a trap of either pride, or conversely, a sense of failure and discouragement. "I'd be glad to." Jacob assured him.

"By the way," Dylan said, "Kaitlin told me what the fifth step is she'd add to my plan to be objective."

"Really? What is it?"

"To see things the way God sees them. She said not only is God's view perfect, but it covers stuff like love."

"Brilliant!"

Dylan said, quietly, "I asked Kaitlin to lunch at the Burger Barn. She said yes." He added shyly, "It's a date."

Jacob grabbed Dylan's hand and shook it. "You be kind to her."

"I will."

Jacob said, "Life is good."

"Yeah," Dylan said. A pause and a smile. "God is good."

The Safe Place

Central Florida—1985

Without love, everything else means nothing . . .

Paraphrase—Apostle Paul, the Bible

THE MONTHLY get-together / luncheon of the Interfaith Council of UCF had been called to order by Rabbi David Fischer, the current rotating head of the group.

At the moment, Father Jack O'Brien, the Newman Center chaplain, was holding forth on Southern names. Father Jack, stout and balding, age 71, had moved from Boston to Florida two years ago for the sake of his lungs. This amused his friends, as he could talk non-stop, revealing no lung incapacity. Happily, Father Jack was always fun to listen to.

"I remember watching a Miss America contest," he said. "The winner was from Georgia, and her name was something like Mary Lou Sue Beth, and she mentioned her boyfriend, Billy Joe Ray Bob. Who has names like that! Sure, we Catholics have confirmation names, but we don't use them all!" He laughed his huge baritone laugh.

"And girls can have their father's name as part of theirs. I have a Mary Michael in my Tuesday group." Jack smiled. "Actually, that's a pretty nice custom."

Jacob liked Father Jack. Jacob had heard from several students that Father Jack really cared about them, and often expressed it. At an orientation cookout, one girl had said to Jacob, "I like it that I can call him Father. He really is like a loving dad."

The Catholic priest was one of the 'old guys' in the group. Even at 41, Jacob was still one of the younger chaplains. In an interesting way, Jacob liked the fact that he was not likely to appreciably change Father Jack's theology. While there were aspects of the Catholic faith Jacob did not agree with, Father Jack's view of Jesus was biblically solid.

"It's all about Him," Jack had said one day to Jacob, pointing to the figure on the crucifix in his office.

"It is," Jacob had replied. "What do priests say instead of 'Amen!'?"

Jack said, "I don't think we say anything." Then he added, somewhat cryptically, "I'm an Augustinian, you know . . . "

The get-togethers of the Interfaith Council could not be called 'meetings,' as it was tacitly agreed upon to avoid any serious religious discussions. The multi-denominational, multi-religion makeup of the council recommended itself to that agreement. Nevertheless, it was enjoyable and a chance for Jacob, hopefully, to plant gospel seeds among his co-ministers. Other than Rabbi Fischer's Judaism, and an interesting young man representing the Baha'i faith, all the chaplains were from some form of Christianity, though several had long since dispensed with the Bible as a truth source.

Jacob's membership in this odd little group was a matter of some necessity. When his work on campus had been under the auspices of Doug Cohan, he had been accorded the credentials of a recognized church. But Doug and Rhonnie had been reassigned by their denomination to a larger church in Raleigh, North Carolina. Doug was to be the associate pastor. This was an agonizing move for the Cohans, because Doug feared the routine of a large church pastor, including the 'hatch, match, and dispatch' duties—christenings, weddings, and funerals—would pull him away from evangelism and personally helping people grow in faith.

So Jacob had formed a new, tiny ministry he called simply 'Life Ministry.' A CPA friend had advised him to incorporate the ministry, so anyone who contributed financially could be issued a tax-deductible receipt. Jacob had resisted the idea initially, as he felt anyone who wanted to give to what he was doing, wouldn't care about getting a tax break. But the CPA, a godly, knowledgeable woman from church, said, "It's the proper way to do it."

And, as an incorporated organization, even composed of only one person, Life Ministry was recognized as an official campus ministry at the

University of Central Florida, formerly known as FTU. Jacob therefore found himself a chaplain member of the Interfaith Council.

During the past ten years, Jacob had often reflected on his decision to leave the teaching job at Drayton to go into ministry. He was glad God had given him a peace about doing so, for he loved the campus work. Jacob felt he was honoring God by sharing the gospel and discipling the few who were hungry. The very nature of this kind of ministry—meeting one to one for an extended period of time to establish a young believer—meant the number of students involved was always small. As Doug Cohan had once said, there was little glory in this for anyone other than God.

Dylan Cooper and Kaitlin had married after graduating, and had two children: Ashley, seven; and Charles, five.

Dylan was an engineer with a large avionics corporation not far from Drayton, and taught an occasional electrical engineering course at the college as an adjunct professor. And, to Jacob's joy, Dylan had kept the ministry at the college going.

Jacob drove the two hours to see Kaitlin and Dylan a couple of times a month. He had a fascinated curiosity about watching the children grow up. He didn't know if they'd be as handsome and beautiful as their mother, but they were certainly smart. When Charles was just shy of five years old, he was sketching figures on a pad when Jacob visited.

"What're the pictures of?" Jacob had asked.

"An underwater camera," Charles replied very seriously. "If I put the camera in a clear box, I have to figure out a way to click the button. If I put the camera in a soft plastic bag, it's easy to take a picture, but it leaks more. And the pictures aren't very good."

"What's the best way, do you think?"

"Put it in a hard box. You can put the lens right on a plastic window, so pictures are good. And I think it's easy to make a little arm to push the button."

Dylan nodded approval. "I agree, Charles. That's a good design."

Kaitlin shook her head, and said, "Engineers!" But the fondness in her voice was evident.

Dylan referred to his daughter as the world's nicest kid, not directly to her, but he made sure she heard his words to Jacob. "And she's diplomatic,"

Kaitlin said, recalling a time when Ashley was looking with delight in her mother's jewelry box. The little girl had sighed, and said, "One day these will all be . . . " Kaitlin laughed. "She was going to say, 'One day, these will all be mine,' but she stopped, looked mournful, and said, 'When sadness comes . . . '"

The Coopers were a pleasure to be around. Dylan's role as an adjunct instructor *and* his going to student apartments on evangelism presented no conflict. For one thing, Dean Brenson had left Drayton to become president of a small college in upstate New York. Another reason was that Dylan's classes were introduction-to-engineering courses with more than a hundred students in a lecture hall. He didn't even know most of their names, much less who were Christians, so the issue of favoritism was irrelevant.

Bible studies at Jacob's house usually meant at least three hours of pool, foosball, pizza, and just hanging out, as well as time in the Word. A local church had upgraded its youth room, and given Jacob its battered foosball and pool tables. The derelict condition of both was a positive. Students didn't have to be careful about rough or, in the case of foosball, violent play.

"Five, four, three, two, one . . . go!" Seth was timing Andrea in a crazy invented game called 'Speed Carnival Pool.'

"Ow," yelled Andrea as she collided with the corner of the pool table. At about five foot, nothing, tiny waif Andrea wasn't built for speed. "I wasn't ready!" The goal of Speed Carnival Pool was to race around the table, sinking the striped balls as fast as possible. The record was an astonishing 22 seconds.

"Okay, start again."

"Hey, no fair," Spencer complained. "You didn't give me a do-over."

"You didn't bat your eyelashes at me."

"Neither did I!" Andrea protested.

"Wait, wait, wait. Okay, Andrea, go . . . now!"

Andrea sank the first ball she aimed at, but then missed the next three. "Rats!" Andrea shouted, as close to cussing as she ever came. She put her hand over her mouth and glanced guiltily at Jacob. "Sorry."

"Six minutes, eleven seconds," Seth said. "It's a new record . . .for you."

The group was doing a series of Bible studies titled '10 Hot Topics.' These included issues such as *Conflict Resolution, How to Know God's Will, Does Prayer Really Work?* and the current topic: *What's the Bible Say About Great Guy-Girl Relationships?* (Sub-title: *How to Date Biblically.*)

The group was five guys and four girls. Two of the guys had been brought to the Bible study by their girlfriends. The topic on dating was definitely timely and challenging.

"What's this Timothy verse actually mean?" Ryan asked. He was Savannah's boyfriend, and he was obviously struggling with the Bible's guidelines for dating. He was, in Jacob's optimistic assessment, a 'pre-Christian.'

"Well, what's it say?" Jacob asked.

"To treat younger women as sisters,"

"And . . . ?"

"In all purity." Ryan added.

"Do you have any sisters, Ryan?"

"One. She's three years older than me."

Jacob asked, "Do you guys ever do stuff together? Like going to movies, or, I don't know, bowling?"

"Sure. What's the point?"

"But you wouldn't make out with her after the movie, right?"

"Eww, that's gross!"

"I think that's what the verse in Timothy is getting at. Guys can have fun around girls, and get to know them, without getting physical. There's another thing in 1 Thessalonians that says men should be sexually honorable, or they could be immoral with a woman who'd might end up being someone else's wife."

"What? I don't get it."

"Let's say I was dating a girl and got physical with her. And years later, I saw her at a college reunion, and she was married. If I'm a Christian, I don't want to have to think, 'I had sex with that man's wife . . . ' The Bible says we should not defraud our brother in this way."

"Okay, okay, I get it. But this is really different than how most people think."

"Yup. You're right about that."

Savannah looked uncomfortable too, and Jacob felt there was some serious reflection going on about their relationship.

The other boyfriend / girlfriend couple, Kimberly and Daniel, had been coming to Bible study for months now, and had dealt with the same issue. They had been leaders in their church's youth group back home in Illinois, yet had been living together off-campus as UCF students. No one had ever talked with them about sexual purity. Jacob had been overjoyed with their response to the Bible's leading; Daniel immediately got an apartment of his own, with three other guys. They had cut out the physical stuff, and Kimberly said that since then, she felt their relationship was better than ever.

'Why are Christians so afraid to share truth?' Jacob wondered. He guessed it was a combination of not knowing what the Bible said, and fear of 'judging' anyone else's behavior.

"Ryan, you've brought up a good point. The way most people see things like this, and what the Bible says is true, can be pretty different."

"That's for sure."

"I think Christians have to be willing to be different, but it has big benefits. God doesn't lay down rules to torment people, but to help them."

Ryan didn't say anything, but Jacob was glad to see that he didn't look defensive, just thoughtful.

Now Justin joined in. Justin was the guy in the group with the most church background, and was a natural leader. He was the defensive co-captain of the UCF football team. And although Jacob knew the Scripture in 1 Corinthians 1 that stated, *God has chosen the weak things of the world to shame the things which are strong . . .* he couldn't help being glad over the credibility that such a cool guy as Justin gave to the group, and Life Ministry.

Justin said, "And there's that verse in, I think, 1 Corinthians, that says we shouldn't be unequally yoked, like believers with unbelievers."

"It's 2 Corinthians 6," Andrea said, with a bit of attitude. For some reason, Andrea found it easy to be irritated by Justin.

"Oh, yeah. Right. " Justin laughed. "The old King James Bible says 'yoked,' and I remember it that way because my youth pastor used to say, 'Don't provoke an unequal yoke.'"

"What do you mean?"

"Well, if the idea is not to be joined together with a non-Christian, then don't date one. That'd be 'provoking' an unequal yoke."

"Thanks. Good discussion, everybody!" 'Hard core stuff!' Jacob thought. 'This will sure get some reactions.'

Jacob closed the Bible study session with prayer, and mentioned that next week's topic was the Bible's teaching on homosexuality. He silently hoped there would be no soul-searching on this one.

*

Jacob had bought a ramshackle house for a cheap price four years ago. In realtor terms, it was somewhere between a 'fixer-upper' and a 'burner-downer.' Its huge advantage was that it was close to campus, in a neighborhood that the realtor said was, "Quite a nice subdivision—once." She put the condition of the house this way, "It certainly has some issues, but the bones are good."

And Jacob had been surprised to learn that he really liked handyman work. Home Depot had how-to books on every conceivable type of home repair: electrical, plumbing, wallboard repair, even bricklaying and concrete block construction. Jacob had bought a bunch of the books, and was slowly getting the old run-down house in good shape.

Seth, a senior accounting major, joined Jacob in working on the house when he could. Like Jacob, he enjoyed the hands-on satisfaction of fixing things.

"Do you need to twist the wires together before you screw the wire cap on?" Seth asked. He was now helping Jacob rewire outlets in the small bedroom.

"The book says 'no, you don't have to,' but I do anyway."

"I like how logical construction is, especially the electrical part." Seth said. "It's kind of like accounting. It just makes sense."

Jacob asked, "So, do you have any jobs lined up for when you graduate?"

"Not in the Orlando area. But there's a good firm in Atlanta I have an interview with next month."

"Ah . . . " Jacob didn't say anything, but he was disappointed to hear that Seth would probably not stay around and get more ministry training. Jacob's goal in ministry had been simply, but compellingly, defined by Jesus' words in Matthew 9. Jesus had seen multitudes of people and had compared them to a field of crops, saying, *The harvest is plentiful, but the workers are few. Pray that the Lord of the harvest would send out workers into His harvest.* Jacob saw that goal, to help people become life-long workers for God, as the ultimate contribution of his life. This tied in perfectly with the aim of keeping people out of the lake of fire. More workers for God meant more people would be saved.

And Seth and Justin were his key guys, who showed the most potential to be workers in God's harvest. Both guys were each helping a younger Christian student grow in his faith.

Jacob had learned from years in ministry that there were no short cuts in helping a person develop the abilities and commitment to serve God whole-heartedly for the long haul.

Several weeks earlier, he and Seth and Justin had camped in a state park for the weekend. It was a fun time of talking, praying together, and trying to figure out how to put the tent up.

"Jacob, where'd you get this thing? It's huge!" Seth was trying to spread out a vast piece of nylon that seemed to be fighting back. It was raining, which made things more challenging.

"It's from a yard sale. The box said it's a family tent that sleeps two adults and four kids. I guess that's why there's two rooms in it."

Justin said, very emphatically, "Okay, here's a universal truth I've discovered about camping. I'm serious. It *always* rains when you're putting the tent up, and it *always* rains when you're taking it down. Even if it only rains twice total for a week, it'll be when the tent goes up and comes down. There are *no* exceptions to this rule. That way the tent and the people inside are always wet."

Jacob smiled at this. It was classic Justin . . . whimsical and dramatic.

"What're these?" Seth asked. He held up a handful of tangled wire cords.

"Not a clue," Jacob said. "But I think those four poles are the corners. Maybe those're tie downs."

Seth said, "Come on, Justin, you're tall. Get under this thing and lift it up. I'll put the corner poles in."

"I'll watch and encourage you on with prayer," Jacob said piously.

Justin's 'universal truth' proved to be true, for when they finally got the tent into some kind of habitable condition, the rain stopped suddenly.

"I knew it!" Justin yelled at the sky.

The next morning, Justin cooked a huge breakfast: scrambled eggs, sausage, and hash browns.

"I'm impressed," Seth said.

"Learned how to cook from the linebacker coach. He was a fanatic on giant breakfasts during summer sessions."

Jacob noticed that even though Justin was probably three inches taller and 50 pounds heavier than Seth, both guys ate the same amount—a lot!

For most of the day, the three of them hiked trails, swam in one of Florida's ice-cold springs; and talked about school, football, their families, and future plans. That evening the guys built a campfire that quickly morphed into a bonfire. Recent high winds had broken small limbs off trees near the campsite, and Seth and Justin proved once again the principle that if a fire is hot enough, it'll burn anything, including green wood.

Jacob had prayed for weeks for a good opportunity to talk seriously with Justin and Seth about being committed to ministry. Sitting at a distance from the intense heat of the fire, Jacob decided this was an ideal time.

'Oh, Lord,' Jacob prayed silently, 'please give me the right words to let these guys know the joy, and the costs, of serving You wholeheartedly.'

"So, guys, let me throw out some thoughts, and see what you think."

Justin and Seth looked at each other, as though they knew this camping trip, with just the three of them, was for a special reason.

Jacob began, "How's it going with Spencer and Danny?" These were the two students Seth and Justin were helping in their Christian faith.

Justin said immediately, "Great! Danny's spending time in the Word, and he said he'd go with me to apartments to share, even though he's pretty nervous about doing that."

"Ah, good for him." He looked at Seth. "How's Spencer doing, Seth?"

Seth frowned. "I don't know. He just doesn't seem that interested. I mean, he's good with reading the Bible and praying when we get together, but when it's just him, it doesn't happen very often." He glanced at Justin, then added. "I don't know how it is with Justin and Danny, but I think that because Spencer and I are about the same age, he doesn't really see me as his teacher. Not like with you and me, Jacob."

"What do you think, if you were ten years older, would it make any big difference with Spencer?"

Seth thought for a moment. "Probably not. I think he likes the group and being part of the stuff we do, but it just doesn't seem like there's any real, I don't know, inner drive about him and the Lord. Honestly, I'm not sure what to do to help him be more serious, like about his faith . . . or if that's even possible."

"Justin, any thoughts about Spencer?"

"I don't know Spencer real well. Like Seth said, he seems to really enjoy hanging out with the group. But he doesn't come with us on evangelism to apartments, and I know Seth has asked him. Do some guys just not want to get to know God better?"

Jacob asked, "What do you mean?"

"I mean, maybe for some people, their main relationship is with the other people in the group, and not so much their relationship with God. My dad says there are folks who are more like 'churchians' than Christians."

"That's probably right," Jacob said. "Obviously, not every Christian is going to be serious. I'm sorry, Seth, if Spencer's like that. But hang in there with him. It could change."

"Yeah, I know. I'm just discouraged."

"I'm not really sure about this," Jacob said, "but it just seems there's a time when something happens in some people, like an ignition in their hearts. It's a tipping point. From that point on, they get serious. There's still the sin and issues, but their heart is committed."

"I hope that happens with Spencer," Seth said.

Jacob got up and threw another two logs on the fire. He sat back down and smiled at the guys. He said, very seriously, "I really appreciate what you both are doing with Spencer and Danny. Sometimes we just don't know how it's going to turn out. Even Paul was puzzled and concerned about some people he was trying to minister to." Jacob paused. "But I think it's always worthwhile—pure gold actually—to invest yourself in others. It's really up to God how it comes out in the long term. I don't think we can ever honestly say, 'Well, that was a waste of time!'"

"Even if the guy you've poured into bails on you?

"Yeah, even then."

Seth smiled. "I'm glad to hear you say that. I *needed* to hear that!"

Here we go, Jacob thought. "So, Seth and Justin, do you see yourselves doing this kind of ministry long-term, like the next fifty years?"

Justin laughed. Seth didn't.

"Seth, let me ask you. In spite of Spencer's issues, do you feel that it was worth it for you to help him?"

Seth said, "Yeah, I do. I mean, I wish he was further along, but he's probably doing better than he'd be doing if we hadn't gotten together. He's not looking at dirty magazines anymore."

Jacob nodded. "Boy, praise God for that! I think that's what's so good. Even if the guys we're helping aren't where we wish they were, they're still helped, and sometimes helped a lot. Even if Spencer never catches fire for Christ, he's still gonna have a better marriage and family."

Justin joined in. "The reason I laughed was the fifty year thing. Jacob, did you think we're going to stop sharing the gospel, or helping guys?"

"I sure hope not. But let's be real. I've seen a lot of people involved in campus ministry stop when they graduate. It's like marching band. Do it in college, then hang up the uniform when they leave. I've seen that happen with ministry."

"Nope," Justin said. "Ain't gonna happen. This stuff is too good to hang up."

Jacob said, "Okay, let me play angel's advocate here. Say you get a great job in, I don't know, Tall Deer, Montana. Either of you. There're two churches there, and neither one has any tradition of lay people actually doing ministry. I mean like evangelism and disciplemaking; I don't mean painting the parsonage, which is probably called ministry. There *is* a branch of Montana State University at Tall Deer: MSUTD, with about 1500 students. You'd be basically on your own. Can you still do this kind of ministry if no one else is, or even if the church folks don't like it that you are?"

"I think I could," Justin said. "In fact, I'd love that!"

"I don't know, " Seth said, honestly. "I hope I'd keep going, but I'm not really a pioneer type. I like to be on a team, and I just don't know if I could build a team from scratch."

Seth looked disheartened, and Jacob quickly jumped in. "Yeah, that's a good insight, Seth."

"I'll have to think about that," Seth said.

The next morning, as they were pulling the tent down, the rain began. Even Justin looked unsettled. "Sorry, Lord," he said. "I was just kidding . . . "

*

A month later, Father Jack showed up at Jacob's house at eight o'clock in the morning. Jacob offered him coffee, which he gladly accepted.

"Some theologians speculate," Father Jack commented solemnly, "that coffee was the only plant God called 'good.' All the rest, like vegetables, came after the fall of mankind."

Jacob smiled. "I didn't know that, Jack. You're a fund of knowledge."

"It's a little known historical fact." He spread his hands out dramatically. "Well, it's not historical, or a fact, but it *is* little known."

"You're pretty coherent for this early."

"Getting up early is kind of a carry-over from seminary days." Jack put his cup down, and folded his hands, as if to pray. Jacob had seen him do this before. It usually meant Jack had something serious on his mind.

"Jacob, there're a couple of guys I'd like to pass along to you, Conner and Eric. They're in my Saturday morning group. Conner's pre-med and Eric's an art major."

"Why have them switch groups?"

"Both of them're making real headway spiritually," Jack said, "and I think they'd benefit from your approach to ministry. I mean, you're more structured, like with Bible study and the evangelism thing." Then he added, "And maybe you could get some individual time with them too."

"Sure. I'd love to meet them, and I'll pray about it. Of course, anyone is welcome to come to Bible study and any activity we do. Did they ask you about coming to our group?"

"Not really. It was my idea. But I mentioned it to them and they seemed interested." Jack paused for a long moment. "Here's the deal, Jacob. Conner is homosexual. Of course, he's not *being* immoral. He's a solid believer. But that's his background. Are you okay with that?"

"Ah." Jacob wasn't sure what to say. This had never come up before in his ministry. And in his heart of hearts, Jacob *did* have a problem with it. He was aware Father Jack was watching him very closely.

"Better tell me what you're thinking," Jack said kindly.

"Oh, Jack . . . of course I'm glad to help anyone who loves the Lord, and wants to grow. It's just I've always had—well, I might as well say it to be honest with you—a repulsion about that. The Romans 1 description: 'men burned in their desire for one another, men with men committing indecent acts' it's just difficult for me."

"I understand."

"Really?"

Jack nodded. "Yes, really." He said nothing further.

Jacob asked, "I guess the question is, are *you* okay with me getting with these guys?"

"I am."

"Okay, then."

"How about if I pick you up at 7:30 tonight, and we'll go meet them?"

"Yeah." Then Jacob said, "Thanks, Jack."

Conner lived in the honors dorm on campus. He was studying chemistry when Jack and Jacob arrived, and said he was glad to take a break. He had dark hair and dark eyes and an intense expression. During the entire visit, Jacob didn't see Conner smile once. He was tall and very thin; Jacob guessed at least six, three.

"It's good to meet you, Jacob," Conner said. "Father Jack has mentioned you quite a few times."

"Hopefully in a good way," Jacob offered the usual cliché.

"Of course," Conner said seriously. "He said your ministry is strong on Bible and discipleship. So Eric and I told Father Jack that we'd like to get your help, if that's good with you."

"It sure is. Is Eric here? Is he your roommate?"

"No. Eric lives in Shannon Apartments, just north of campus. Do you want to go meet him too? We can walk there."

"Yeah. Great."

Eric came to the door of his apartment with paint on his hands and face. Physically, it would be hard to imagine a greater contrast to Conner. Pale and short, but here again, the expression was solemn.

"Sorry about the paint. Come on in."

Father Jack introduced Jacob, and Jacob asked, "What're you painting?"

Conner answered for him. "You won't believe this. He is *such* a great painter. Is that Glenn's mother's portrait?"

"Yeah. It's almost done." Eric turned an easel toward them.

Jacob was very impressed with the professionalism of the portrait. It was of a fifty'ish woman and was both beautiful and realistic.

Conner said, with pride in his voice, "Eric does portraits as a part time job. And he doesn't charge near enough."

Eric did smile at the compliment. "It pays for the oils." He was friendly during their visit, but said very little, even when Father Jack asked about how he'd started painting. He seemed to be looking at Jacob studiously, as though evaluating how he'd paint Jacob's portrait. It was a bit unnerving for Jacob.

As they left Eric's apartment, Jacob glanced back and saw that Eric was watching them leave from his apartment window..

"Interesting guy," Jacob said. "He's sure talented."

"Yes," Conner commented. "I remember reading that da Vinci dissected bodies to learn how to paint people realistically. From my anatomy classes, I'd say Eric has a kind of God-given ability to see people's bone and muscle structure accurately too. His portraits are good, and he earns money that way, but his other stuff is amazing."

"How so?" Father Jack asked.

"It's realistic, not abstract, and it's all people, but he just instills such deep feeling in the expresions. It's hard to explain. Ask him sometime to show you his painting of old people."

"Where're he get models to do old people?"

Conner stopped walking. "You know, I don't know. I never asked."

Jacob said. "It'll be great to have you guys in Bible study. And we can do some other things too, like evangelism, if you're up for it."

"I am," Conner said.

'He *almost* smiled . . . ' Jacob thought. 'This'll be challenging for us both.'

So Conner and Eric began coming to Jacob's college Bible study. Conner participated in the discussions with carefully thought-out ideas. Eric appeared to enjoy being in the study group, smiling and nodding in agreement with other's comments, but rarely uttering a single word himself.

Justin teased Eric about his old pickup truck, which Justin nicknamed the 'shipwreck' because it leaked so much oil. Justin suggested filling the back of the truck with sand, then drilling holes in the truck bed so Eric would spread sand on the dripping oil as he drove. Eric took the teasing with good humor. But Jacob felt that despite Eric's friendliness, he was a difficult person to get to know. There was just something about Eric that made Jacob uncomfortable. For one thing, Eric always wore long sleeved shirts, which made Jacob wonder if he'd done serious drugs in the past.

The great exception to Eric's silence in the Bible study group came during a prayer time at the end of a study on how to serve God.

"What are some prayer requests tonight?" Jacob asked. He always hoped students would ask God for someone they could disciple, or share Christ with. Invariably, however, to Jacob's frank annoyance, there was someone who wanted prayer for an aunt's arthritic knee, or, that most cliché of all prayer requests, 'traveling mercies' for some cousin driving to Atlanta.

The very first prayer request was from Stephanie, a community college student who was the shiest person in the group. "Would someone pray for my bunny. He's really sick." Stephanie was visibly upset. "His name is Fluffy," she said quietly.

Jacob thought, 'Oh, good grief. Fluffy the bunny!'

But when the time to pray came, Eric got up, sat down next to Stephanie, and, surprisingly, held her hand. He prayed, "Oh, dear Father, please heal Fluffy. He's your gentle creature, and Stephanie says he's really sick.

Please give Stephanie peace about her rabbit. I pray that Fluffy will be much better by the time Stephanie goes home tonight. Please, Jesus, make Stephanie's sweet bunny all better. Amen."

Jacob was moved by the simple beauty of Eric's prayer. And he was a little uneasy with his own callousness about the bunny prayer request.. 'It's not about Fluffy,' he thought. 'It's about Stephanie.'

As if reading his thoughts, Conner nodded at Jacob, and actually smiled.

Conner began going with Jacob to student apartments near campus. Serious as ever, he was nevertheless relaxed and relational with students. College students usually appeared to enjoy responding to the little survey, and at least half the time, agreed to seeing the gospel illustration.

One evening, Conner and Jacob were talking to a guy with spike hair and a T-shirt picturing of a bowl of vegetables screaming 'Salads Are Murder!' Conner asked him what he'd change about religion if he could change anything. The answer was, "Stop being judgmental."

"Okay. About what kind of things?"

"Christians are very judgmental about gays." Then he added, "I'm gay. So you guys probably think I'm headed straight for hell."

Conner said simply, "I'm gay too. And I'm not going to hell."

There was a shocked silence for a moment. Then the student said, "Are you serious? Are you really gay? And you're a Christian?"

"Yes. Can I share what the Bible says on this? I'd like to hear your thoughts."

The student looked skeptical. "The Bible talks about being gay?"

"Well, yeah, but that's not what I want to show you. Here, let me draw a fast picture."

Jacob had told Conner about Doc Yoder's use of Hebrews 11:6 to share with agnostics, that God rewards those who seek Him. Conner had come up with a quick illustration starting with that Scripture. He called the illustration 'HeRo John' with three verses from Hebrews, Romans, and John, that the reward is Christ dying for their sins, and that whoever accepts Jesus is a child of God.

Conner shared this with this student—whom Jacob had named in his mind, 'Spike.'

"So that's it. The whole thing hinges on whether a person thinks what they're doing is wrong. I did. That's when I became a Christian."

"So, really, you're not gay," Spike said. "Not now."

Conner answered seriously, "That's another whole issue." He looked Spike right in the eyes. "Please think about this. If, in your heart, you think how you're living is wrong, ask Christ to forgive you, and He will."

Spike didn't say a word. He looked confused. Later Conner told Jacob that the confusion was a good sign, that it meant Spike's defenses were down, and there would be a moment when he wouldn't quickly rationalize his sin. "It only takes a few seconds of vulnerability for a guy like that to come to Christ." Conner said. "I know." Then he added, "Some day I'll tell you what Father Jack shared with me, that made all the difference. It's how I came to Christ."

As they left Spike's apartment, it began to rain hard. Jacob and Conner ran to the car.

"Let's call it a day, for apartments," Jacob said.

"Yes. I think you'd probably like to talk about that last guy, and what I shared with him."

"Yeah, definitely."

"I know Father Jack told you about me. About where I'm coming from. So you weren't surprised when I told that guy I was gay."

"Can we call him 'Spike'? That's what I named him in my brain . . .“

Conner looked relieved, and laughed. "Super appropriate. Spike it is." He paused. "So *did* it surprise you, Jacob, when I said I was gay to Spike?"

"No, not really. Maybe just a little caught off guard. We haven't discussed this these past few weeks. I didn't know if I should bring it up."

"Then it was good it came up tonight."

Jacob asked, "What did you mean when Spike said, 'So you're not gay, now,' and you said that was another whole issue? I don't get that."

Conner took a deep breath. "Okay. I'm glad we can talk about this. Maybe you can give me some insight on something in Scripture I'm not sure about."

"Go ahead."

"First of all, I know homosexuality is wrong. I'm a Christian. I know and believe the Bible. Romans 1 says that those who practice such things are worthy of death. I believe that's true"

Conner opened his little New Testament. "I didn't always believe that. For years I just thought if there was a God, He'd made me this way. But that can't be true, because if He'd *made* gays that way, He couldn't very well say they were worthy of death."

He turned to First Corinthians, chapter 6. "Here's what I don't understand. I'm sure you know this passage. Verses nine through eleven say, *Don't be deceived; neither fornicators, nor adulterers, nor effeminate, nor homosexuals, nor thieves, nor the covetous, nor drunkards, nor revilers, nor swindlers, shall inherit the kingdom of God. And such were some of you; but you were washed, but you were sanctified, but you were justified in the name of the Lord Jesus Christ, and in the Spirit of our God."*

"What's the part you don't understand?" Jacob asked.

"The NIV Bible uses the phrase 'sexually immoral' instead of fornicators in verse nine. As distinct from homosexuals. So obviously, straight-sex sin, including adultery, is wrong too."

"Of course. That's very clear. Along with all the other sins in that list."

"What I don't understand is this. When it says, 'and such *were* some of you, but you're washed, you're sanctified . . . ' what does that mean? Does that mean that *now* homosexuals no longer feel attraction to men? Or, does it mean that because of being in Christ, now we don't *act* immorally?"

"Conner, is this what you meant when you told Spike it was another issue as to whether you were still gay?"

Conner said "yes," and looked sad. "Jacob, when I came to Christ, I know He forgave all my sins, but I didn't instantly become a heterosexual. I didn't go from gay to straight.

"Oh, man, it's so difficult," he said. "I'm still attracted to men. That's my temptation. But I know that temptation itself isn't sin if you don't give in to it. And I don't."

"I agree," Jacob said. He thought for a moment. "First chapter of Peter says, *like the Holy One who called you, be holy yourselves in all your behavior.* So it seems like our behavior's important. I'd include our thought life too."

"Okay," Conner said assertively, "here's what I've thought out. Jacob, you're straight, and, I assume, tempted to lust after women. You fight to be moral—no lust, no self-gratification, no immoral sex, not even immoral thoughts. Jesus said if a man lusts after a woman, it's as bad as having sex with her. Right?"

"Right."

"Okay. I'm still tempted to lust after men. And my fight is the same as yours, to be moral. No lust, no masturbation, no sex with men, or even thinking about it."

Jacob was impressed with how seriously Conner took holiness. He closed his eyes to concentrate. "Where's the verse that says, 'Jesus was tempted in every way we are, but He didn't sin' . . .?"

Conner smiled and said, "It's Hebrews 4:15. I've got all the verses nailed down on this topic."

"So, we agree temptation isn't sin."

"Yes. But what I struggle with is, whether my being tempted by attraction to men is somehow wrong."

"Conner, I don't know. I do know God isn't the author of confusion. So let's agree to this: temptation is not sin unless we give in to the temptation. Victory is victory! Victory over sexual temptation comes from Christ. Paul said to the Corinthians, who were pretty much sexually crazy, that God will always provide a way of escape from temptation."

"Good. Thanks, Jacob." Conner's expression was the most encouraging Jacob had ever seen on his face.

A thought abruptly struck Jacob, and he threw it out. "Let me ask you something about Eric. Is he gay?"

Conner looked shocked. "No. Of course not. Did you think he was?"

"I don't know. There's just something I feel kind of uncomfortable about with Eric. And . . . I wondered if he'd done heroin."

"Because of the long sleeves?"

"Yeah,"

Conner looked out the side window of Jacob's car for several moments, and seemed to come to a decision. He turned back to Jacob. "This is just between us, Jacob. I mean really confidential. When Eric was thirteen, he cut his wrists."

"Oh., Lord . . . he tried to kill himself?"

"Yes. He's still pretty fragile, but he's not gay."

'Dear God', Jacob thought, 'life really is hard.'

"Thanks, Conner. Thanks for talking with me tonight."

"So," Conner said seriously, "would you want to have some accountability with each other? About how we're doing with staying holy sexually?"

"Aha! You mean the kind where we agree not to lie?"

Conner laughed and nodded. "Yeah. We agree not to lie, and how about two more things: no details and no preaching. If you ask me, how I'm doing, all I'll say is either 'good,' or 'not so good,' and I won't give any details. And you can't preach at me about doing better. What do you think?"

"Let's do it."

"Rain's stopped. Do you want to go back to the apartments and share with people?"

"Nah," Jacob said. "Time for me to head home. Lots to think about."

Eric also came out with Jacob to student apartments. As he always did with 'rookies,' Jacob assured Eric that he didn't have to do anything, that Jacob would take care of the entire conversation with whomever they were talking to. Eric seemed comfortable being along with Jacob as they talked with students. He told Jacob how good he thought the survey approach was, and how impressed he was with Jacob's gospel presentation. The third time Eric came out, and a guy opened the door of his apartment, Jacob handed the little clipboard with the survey forms to Eric. "Eric, why don't you ask our survey questions?"

Suddenly, Eric's expression changed. He looked startled. He took the clipboard, and asked the survey questions, but appeared very nervous, even fearful.

It was the last time Eric went with Jacob on evangelism. In the coming weeks, Eric always had a good reason why he wasn't able to go out. Jacob was disappointed. He decided he'd do a pretty hard-core Bible study on commitment for the group. Jacob had an increasing sense of urgency for young Christians to decide whether they would serve God, or not. 'The workers in the harvest are *still* few,' Jacob thought, 'and so many students seem content to just drift along.'

He mentioned his plan for a 'commitment' Bible study to Father Jack. Jack even had a joke about lack of Christian commitment. "So, a ship's captain came across a tiny island in the middle of the ocean, and there was a single person living there. The man said he'd been on the island for many years. The captain noticed there were some thatch structures, and asked what they were for.

'This one is my home, where I live,' the man said. 'And this second one is my store, where I keep my supplies. The third one is my church, where I worship.'

'And what's the fourth one,' the captain asked.

'Oh, that's the church I *used* to go to . . . "'

Father Jack roared with laughter. No one enjoyed Jack's jokes more than he did himself! But then he added, on a serious note, " Jacob . . . be careful."

The next week, Jacob had the study on commitment, focusing on the Matthew 9 'workers are few' verses, the Luke 14 passage of counting the cost and being willing to give up everything to serve God, and the sobering verse of Hebrews 10:38, . . . *My righteous one shall live by faith. If he shrinks back, My soul has no pleasure in him.*
Jacob admitted later to himself that he'd probably gotten too impassioned in his conclusion to the study. The group was uncharacteristically quiet.

But overall, Jacob thought the responses were pretty good. Justin was enthusiastic, and afterwards said he thought it was right on target. Justin even said he felt that full-time Christian work was possibly where God was leading him. Jacob couldn't tell what Eric or Conner thought.

The following week, Eric didn't come to Bible study. Conner said he'd check on Eric. Then Conner stopped coming.

After another week, Jacob went to Conner's room on campus, but he wasn't there. When he called Conner, Conner didn't answer, but that was normal for Conner. He'd once told Jacob he often let the phone ring because it might be his parents, and those conversations never went well. He was a hard person to get hold of on the phone.

Jacob tried to see Eric at his apartment one night, but he could see through the window blinds that the apartment was dark. Jacob had a growing awareness that in his own thinking, he'd given up on Conner and Eric. He praised God they were saved, but decided the chances of them being workers for God were slim. Jacob felt both a sense of sadness, but also relief. 'These guys just have too many issues, too much baggage,' he thought.

Father Jack hadn't heard from Conner or Eric either, and he was worried. "Tell me about the teaching you did on being committed."

Jacob told him the Scriptures, and the challenge he'd presented to the group.

Father Jack, gentle-natured as he was, looked troubled. "Wasn't that pretty tough for the younger Christians to hear?"

"But that's what Jesus did. He sure didn't pull any punches. He blasted the Pharisees and even some of His followers with a tough message."

"But Jacob, He was gentle and forgiving with hurting people, like the woman caught in adultery, or the woman at the well."

"What are you saying, Jack?"

"I guess I'm saying you might have scared them away."

"Really? Do you mean it?"

"That last verse . . . someone might see that as, if he doesn't do what *you* want, you wouldn't like him." He paused. "Remember Jesus and the rich young ruler? It said Jesus felt a love for him. The young man didn't do what Jesus wanted, but I don't think Jesus stopped loving him."

Jacob thought hard. Was that how he'd come across?

Jacob said, "Okay, maybe Eric. I can see that. But it doesn't seem like Conner would leave because of that."

"Ah, Jacob," Jack said, "haven't you noticed how protective of Eric Conner is?"

Jacob hadn't. "No, I guess not."

"Well, this'll be a little different for you and me, but let me share some Bible with you, Jacob, that I think—I hope—will help. I didn't hear this in seminary. It was an old friend, an Episcopal priest, who gave me this."

Jacob said. "What's the Scripture?"

"It's 1 Thessalonians, chapter two. I think it summarizes all ministry in three words.

"Look at verse eleven and twelve. That's you. . . . *exhorting and encouraging and imploring each one of you, so that you may walk in a manner worthy of God.* You're a good teacher of the Word, and you're good at exhorting people to walk with God. That's what you did with your challenge to the group about commitment.

"Now look at verse 7. Read it, Jacob."

Jacob read, *"But we proved to be gentle among you, as a nursing mother tenderly cares for her own children."*

"That's me, Jacob. I'm probably not as good as you in teaching and exhorting, but I've learned to love people like a mother. Have you ever seen a mother with a baby?"

"No. Not really."

"She's so gentle and loving. She'll say loving words to a baby who can't understand them, but I'm convinced the baby picks up on the loving heart of his mother. Do you see what I'm saying? Ministry is both, love and truth: the teaching, exhorting heart of the father, and the totally loving, accepting heart of the mother. That's the three words: *love and truth.* People need to know we love them."

Jacob didn't know what to say. Jacob's heart was suddenly fearful. What Jack had shared rang true. "Oh, Jack, what have I done?"

"You've done what you're strong at." Jack smiled. "If we combined you and me, we'd have a perfect minister."

As the Fall term came to a close, with the campus nearly empty for Christmas break, UCF football earned a spot in a post-season bowl game against South Carolina. UCF fought its way to a dramatic 31–30 upset win. Justin played his best game ever, with a recovered fumble and two interceptions, and he was named the game's defensive MVP!

As Jacob congratulated Justin the next day, a very excited Justin had some startling news.

"Jacob, you won't believe this! There was a Miami Dolphins scout at the game, and he offered me a shot at an NFL tryout."

"Really? Are you going to do it?"

"Of course!"

"But you'd said that you felt God was maybe leading you to full-time Christian work."

"And He still might. But, Jacob, this is a once in a lifetime chance. God's given me a gift as an athlete. Think of the testimony for Christ I could have if I got into the NFL."

"Okay."

Justin said, "I'm kind of surprised. I thought you'd be excited about this. I mean, most NFL players only are in the league for maybe ten years. I could sure do ministry after that."

"Well, Justin, I hope it all works out."

"Thanks! I think it will. It'll be great!"

The second surprise that same week came from Seth.

"So Jacob, I've decided to stay in the area for at least next year. I said 'no' to the Atlanta job."

"What? I thought that was a great offer."

"It sure was, money-wise. It was kinda amazing how much they were going to pay me."

"I've got to say, I'm really glad. How'd you decide this?"

Seth said, "The job was good, and exactly what I'd taken the accounting major for; but I think I've changed my perspective. Ministry seems more important now, and the Atlanta people made it pretty clear that they expected their staff to have the firm as the number one priority."

"That's a great insight, Seth." Jacob was rejoicing silently, and couldn't help grinning at this news.

"Plus, I remember you saying one time about being happy you had a good job to give up to serve the Lord." Now Seth smiled. "So, if it's good with you, let's get me really trained for ministry. I especially want to know how to do solid Bible studies, and how to meet one-to-one with guys."

"You got it! Seth, this is great. But how are you going to live, I mean, pay your bills?"

"I took a job with Barbara McKinsey's CPA office. It's not as much as the Atlanta deal, but it'll be plenty."

Barbara was the CPA from church who had helped Jacob set up Life Ministry. Jacob thanked God in his heart for Seth, and thanked Him for this evidence of

God's still entrusting him with the treasure of the Gospel.

*

Jacob sat at the Life Ministry table under his favorite sycamore on campus. At the end of February, it was still cool enough to be comfortable. 'Table'ing' in the heat of summer term was not for the faint of heart. He was reading through the book of Acts again, with the idea of doing a series of Bible studies on the early disciples' activities.

As he looked up, he saw Conner near the front of the library. Jacob jumped up and ran toward Conner. "Conner, man, am I glad to see you!"

There was definitely restraint in Conner's expression and voice. "Jacob . . . sorry I haven't been in touch."

"I'm the one who's sorry, Conner. Father Jack showed me pretty clearly that I'd been a real jerk as far as relating to you and Eric."

"It's okay."

"How is Eric? I've been worried. Hey, and please give Father Jack a call and let him know you're okay."

There was a pause.

"I'm okay, but Eric's had a bad accident."

"What? When? Was he hurt?"

"Yeah. It was a week ago. Lots of cuts and bruises, and some broken ribs. But the worst was a broken femur. It was a compound fracture, where the bone comes through the flesh."

"Oh, dear God. Conner, how'd it happen?"

"Well, he hit a bridge abutment at pretty high speed. The cops think he must have fallen asleep, because there were no skid marks, like he'd been braking."

Conner was watching Jacob closely as he described the accident. "Fortunately, the door of his old truck sprang open and Eric was thrown out. He wasn't wearing a seat belt."

"Eric *always* wears a seat belt."

"Not this time."

Jacob had a sudden sense of something terrible. "It wasn't an accident, was it?"

Conner shook his head.

Jacob choked back an urge to cry. "Oh, Conner. Am I part of this? Did I cause this?"

"No, no. It's way more complicated than that. And it's okay."

"Will Eric be all right?"

"Yes. Sure. But she's still in the hospital. It's going to be a while."

"What?"

"What, what?"

"You said 'she!' You said '*she's* still in the hospital."

Conner turned away from Jacob and rubbed his hand over his eyes. "Ah. Well, it's not really a secret. Eric's friends know. He just didn't want you or Father Jack to know.

"Eric was born a girl. When his mom moved, and he went to a different high school, he changed over to being a guy."

Jacob said, "I don't understand."

"I know you don't."

"Eric is a girl?"

"Eric is who Eric is. This is really hard to explain."

Jacob had a sense of unreality. He even felt a little angry, because he was so confused.

"Try."

"Jacob, his whole life, Eric has just wanted to belong somewhere she was cared about. Yeah, I know, I'll say she every now and then.

"I don't know all about her; I never felt comfortable asking her. But I think her dad left when she was nine or ten. All she's ever said was that she felt safer being a boy. She wants to feel safe."

"Conner, I can't stand this. I've been a part of hurting her . . . What if she tries again."

"No. No she won't. This is the good part. At the last second, she swerved so she hit the bridge in a glancing way, so the truck spun and she was thrown out. When you see her, ask her why she swerved."

"Should I go see her? In the hospital?"

"Oh, yes. You should, for both of your sakes."

"I will."

"Jacob, she doesn't blame you. She certainly doesn't hate you. She just saw in you, like a dad, a hope of the love that she's always yearned for. When she *felt* it wasn't there—that she couldn't please you—she gave up. She's so fragile."

He looked with kindness at Jacob. "Jacob, just have your ministry be a safe place, where people are loved."

Jacob couldn't say anything.

Conner said, "It was kind of sad and funny too. You didn't know how she was. You said you were uncomfortable about Eric and wondered if he was gay. I think you wanted him to be more masculine."

"Oh, God, forgive me."

"Yes. And me too." He didn't explain why he felt a need to be forgiven.

Conner said, "Let's go over to your table. I'll tell you what Father Jack said to me that brought me to Christ."

They sat under the tree. Conner said, "I went with Eric to one of Father Jack's little services at the Newman Center. Afterward, we got talking and I shared with him that I was gay."

"How'd he respond to that?"

"Here's what he said. 'Conner, do you have any straight friends?' I said 'Yes, of course.' Jack asked, 'What if you were dying of, say, kidney disease, and one of your straight friends said, 'Conner, I care about you and I'm willing to donate a kidney to you so you can live.' Would you take it?' I said, 'Yes.' 'Okay,' Father Jack said, 'What if you were dying and you friend said, I'll give you one of my kidneys, but I want you to know that I think homosexuality is wrong. Would you still take the kidney? So you could live?' Jacob, I'll admit, I waited a few seconds, but I said 'Yes, I would.'"

Conner smiled. "It was kind of brilliant. Jack said, 'That's exactly what God does. He doesn't just give a kidney, but His own Son's life, so we can live. God loves us that much. But He *also* tells us the truth about the sin in our lives.' Jack said that idea was hard for people to grasp because most humans are one or the other. They're either judgmental without love, or kindly but without sharing truth."

"And that's how you came to Christ . . . " Jacob said quietly.

"Yes. I asked Christ to forgive me, and to help me have a life that was pleasing to God." He spread his arms out. "That was the whole thing. It's so simple."

"Did you lead Eric to Christ?"

"Yes."

"What's going to happen with Eric now?"

Conner said, "I'm taking care of her." He leaned forward in the folding chair. "I love her."

Jacob was surprised. "What do you mean? I don't understand . . . "

"No, no. Nothing's changed that way, Jacob. But it's kind of wonderful, really. What I mean is, I love her because I care about her so much."

Jacob said, "Conner, thank you. Thank you." Then he asked what he'd been wanting to ask. "What's her name?"

"She's in the big Seventh Day Adventist hospital down town." Conner smiled. "Ask her when you see her."

Jacob sat for a few minutes in the parking garage of the hospital. He prayed, 'Oh, Father, I don't know what to say or do. Please help me.'

Eric was in a private room with close nursing supervision. Her door was partly open; it looked like she was sleeping. Jacob had once visited a church member who'd fractured his femur, and there was a external traction device holding the bone in place. Jacob was grateful to see that Eric didn't have this. Both her legs were covered by a blanket.

Jacob knocked softly on the door. Eric opened her eyes, and—praise God, Jacob thought—smiled.

"Jacob. I'm glad you came."

Jacob said quietly, "Hey, Eric. How are you doing?"

Again, a smile "Not too bad. I've got a rod in my thighbone, and my ribs hurt. But really, I'm doing great."

"Eric, I'm so sorry . . . "

"Don't be. Please. And it's not Eric—now."

"Ah . . . "

"My name is Holly. I'm Holly Mitchell."

"Holly. I like it."

Holly said, "Conner told me you'd talked. You must think this is all pretty weird."

"No, I don't. I'm just so sorry, Holly, for everything. Please forgive me."

"I do." A pause. "Jacob, God used you, and the crash, in my life."

"Well, if that's so, it's sure not the way I'd ever want to be used. Like a trash can in someone's life." Jacob spoke with mocking self-reproach, "'God, thank you for Jacob. He was so unloving, he turned me to You!'"

Holly laughed. "Not quite that drastic."

Jacob said, somewhat nervously, "Conner said I should ask you why you swerved."

Now Holly became serious. "I was so freaked out. I was going to do it. But I heard a voice say, 'No!' and I jerked the wheel."

"Holly, you mean . . . ?"

"That it was God? I'm sure it was. I don't know if it was an actual out-loud word, or if I heard it in my mind. But I knew it was God, and *it was loud.*

"Jacob, it was so clear. It's like for a long time I've wanted for someone who loved me enough, to say, 'No! Don't do that.' And it was God who did."

"I think I get that." Jacob sat down in a chair next to the head of the bed. "Holly, I've got to tell you, it used to bother me that I thought you were too feminine. Now, I'm glad. You're beautiful."

There were tears in her eyes. "Thank you."

"God has used you in my life too, Holly. I'm so sorry I hurt you."

Neither said anything for a moment. Then Holly said, "This hospital is religious. Every room has a framed verse on the wall." She pointed to the verse on her wall, near the door, facing the bed. "Look at the verse for my room."

The framed Scripture said,

> *In Thy presence is fulness of joy.*
> Psalm 16:11

Jacob said, "Yes."

"I think that's what He's always wanted me to know."

She said, "I'm still concerned whether people like me. Even now, I'm worried about what you think of me." Holly smiled the lovely smile. "But not too much."

*

Jacob and Father Jack were drinking coffee at an outdoor table at the *Café Henri* across from campus. Jack, whimsically, had asked to speak to Henri, to compliment him on his coffee. This request had been met, of course, with confused stares. Jack had laughed his huge laugh.

Then Jacob introduced a serious note. "Jack, there was a time there when I really thought I'd disqualified myself from ministering."

"I could see that. And now?"

"I've been doing a study in Acts. When Paul met the Lord on the road to Damascus, he learned that what he'd been doing was wrong. He'd hurt many Christians. But it seemed like he immediately turned his strengths to serving God, and God's people. He was still strong and confident."

"True."

"He didn't dwell in guilt. He accepted God's forgiveness."

"Also true."

"I'm going to do the same."

Father Jack O'Brien said, "Well, this is probably the first time an Augustinian ever said this, but 'Amen, brother!'"

The Honesty of Winter

2019

In the honesty of winter, you see
the crows in your garden and remember
what grew there, where bare branches
clear a line of sight . . .

> "Winter Nights, Falling"—Naming a Stranger
> John Hazard

AS JACOB walked past UCF's reflecting pool, lines of Dylan Thomas came to him. *Do not go gentle into that good night. Old age should burn and rave at close of day.*

Jacob thought, 'I think I'm too tired to burn and rave.' He was going to meet up with Michael Kowalski, nicknamed 'Percy' because he liked to quote from Percy Shelley. Since Percy was a PhD student in English Lit, this was appropriate.

Percy was sitting on the grass in front of the library. "Hey, Jacob, you look thoughtful."

"Ha. Well, I was thinking about a guy from many years ago, and how I could've helped him more."

Percy said, "*We look before and after, we pine for what is not; our sincerest laughter with some pain is fraught . . .*"

"Where's that from?"

"Skylark."

It struck Jacob, as it had many times before, how incongruous it seemed to hear Michael quote Romantic poetry. 'Percy' was, as one guy put it, 'like a stack of cannonballs in a T-shirt.' His powerful build, and frankly intimidating features lent themselves more to the image of a pro wrestler than an English major.

They sat on the grass and reviewed some verses of Scripture they'd been memorizing. Percy liked Romans 1:8 *First, I thank my God through Jesus Christ for you all, because your faith is being proclaimed throughout the whole world.* He'd been very encouraged by some of the students in his Bible study who were trying to share the gospel with their friends.

Jacob had memorized, years ago, a verse in Acts 20 in which Paul said he didn't consider his life as dear to himself, in order that he might finish his course. Now that he was 75, Jacob thought this verse was increasingly relevant. There was a sense of urgency to finish well, but also an increasing weariness.

Perhaps Percy picked up on Jacob's tiredness. With a concerned expression, he said, "Hey, we've got an uneven number for evangelism this evening. Why don't you take a break for tonight."

"Oh, okay. I am tired. Didn't sleep all that great last night."

Then Percy said, "So, I saw this old movie on Netflix a couple of days ago. I know you're not a movie guy, but this movie, *Men In Black*, actually had a Great Commission message in it. Well, sort of."

"Is that the silly one about space aliens?"

"Yeah. The men in black are agents who keep humanity safe from bad aliens. Anyway, there's this one scene where the old guy is explaining to a young recruit all about being a man in black. The young guy asks, 'Why don't we tell the whole country there are aliens? They'd understand. People are smart.' The old agent says, 'A *person* is smart. People are stupid.' Then the agent-to-be asks, 'What's the cost?' The older man says, 'No one will ever know what you're doing. You'll get no praise or recognition.' Then as the older agent gets up and starts walking away, the young guy yells after him, 'Is it worth it?' The old agent turns around and says, 'It is, if you're strong enough.'"

"Ah, okay. Where's the Great Commission?"

"It's the three things. First, individuals are smart, and groups aren't. So, just like we don't try to change groups in ministry, we concentrate on individuals who want to grow."

Jacob smiled. "That's a bit of a stretch."

"And second, the men in black are basically incognito; they get no recognition for saving mankind. Same with disciplemaking. You'll never be famous, Jacob, for all the hours you've help me grow and get trained."

"Now that one, I buy. Real discipleship is usually pretty dinky."

"And finally, the older guy says, 'It's worth it, if you're strong enough.' I think that's really true. It's lonely and hard, this kind of ministry. If we wanted to be popular, we'd stay shallow in people's lives. But that's not really making disciples."

Jacob laughed. "You sure get a lot of philosophy out of movies! Percy, you're wise beyond your years."

As Jacob drove home after his time with Percy, he was saddened to realize he'd felt a sense of relief when Percy suggested he skip evangelism that night. Jacob had always loved to go to college apartments to talk with students about the Lord. Why had he been relieved to *not* go? True, he was tired, but at his age it didn't take much to get tired. And no matter how tired he was, he always got fired up when he was talking with students. 'Please, Lord, don't let me grow weary of something that's pure gold.'

A week later, Jacob was on his way to a rural area north of Orlando to try to track down a Craig's List basketball goal. Suddenly, billows of fog came from the A/C vents on his ancient Honda. Jacob knew it was nothing serious, but he pulled over into a grassy driveway, and turned the engine off for a few minutes. This usually fixed the issue.

He was on a road with no residences or subdivisions, just lots of trees. He noticed a 'Land For Sale' sign with a realtor's number about fifty feet away. It said, '1.6 Acres—High and Dry!'

'Good,' Jacob thought. 'I'm not trespassing.' He got out and walked down the overgrown drive, really just two tire tracks. The lot was mostly pine with a few large oak trees. A few hundred feet in, there was a clearing. He saw a metal deer-hunting stand in one of the oaks, but it was rusted and dilapidated. The land fell off gradually at the back of the property, and Jacob could see through the tall pines for another couple hundred feet.

"What a great spot," Jacob said aloud. Except for the soft sound of a breeze in the tops of the pines, quietness prevailed. To Jacob, who had never lived in the country, the silence was unusual and pleasing. 'This would be such a nice place for camping,' Jacob thought.

As he left, on impulse, he took a photo with his phone of the realtor's sign. He called the Craigs List seller, and said he'd changed his mind about the basketball goal. When he got home, he called Kirken Realty, and spoke to Katherine.

"I'm calling about the lot for sale on Black Oak Road."

"Well," Katherine said, "that was fast. I just put the sign up. I haven't even posted that property online yet. How'd you know about it?"

"I was just driving by it today. What can you tell me about it"

"It's one and a half acres, give or take. Property taxes last year were only 317 dollars, and the asking price is 27 thousand. That's really low for that area, by the way."

Jacob asked, "Is it? Why do you say it's cheap?"

"It's owned by a gentleman," Katherine replied, "who lives in Jacksonville, and only used it for deer hunting."

"Yeah, I saw a tree stand."

"Oh, you've walked around on it?"

"Yes. Hope that was okay. I figured that since there was a realtor sign, it was all right."

"Of course. I'm glad you did. Isn't it nice out there? The cleared quarter acre in the middle is where the owner parked his camper." She continued, "The reason it's cheap is that the county has bought nearly 150 acres to the north of it, that backs right up to the lot. It's now a public, county-owned park, Pine Bluff Preserve. Since there's obviously no more hunting on that land, the owner wants to get rid of it."

"Ah, so there won't be any development to the north then."

"That's right. Sir, if you're interested, take it today. When I post it, it'll go fast. I have a lot to do today, so I won't post it until tomorrow morning, but please let me know what you decide before five o'clock this evening."

Jacob said, "I will. Thank you. You've been very helpful."

All that day, Jacob went back and forth in his mind about the wooded lot. 'This is interesting,' he thought, 'Totally out of the blue. But it would be fun to have a place like that to camp.' He had the money in savings and redeemable CD's. And he had a line of credit at his bank. He could buy it if he wanted.

And he did buy it. Jacob called Katherine at 4 o'clock to tell her. She was pleased, but not surprised, or particularly excited. Her commission on such a low-priced property would not be great. Jacob agreed to meet her in two days at her office. The next day, he put 17 thousand on his bank line of credit, and transferred 12 thousand from his saving account to checking. In three days, he was a land owner 'out in the sticks.'

And this was the start of what Jacob came to think of as his long-delayed mid-life crisis. It wasn't the red Corvette. It was the 1.6 acres of 'high and dry' pine woods.

Jacob found his little popup dome tent and camped on the lot the following weekend. He woke up early Saturday morning. Sipping coffee from the big thermos he'd brought, he watched the sun come up, slanting through the pines. It was peaceful and lovely.

'I should build a deck,' Jacob thought, 'to put a bigger tent on. Eye bolts for the tent corners.' Then another thought occurred to him. 'I wonder if it's legal to dig a deep hole for an outhouse.' He'd have to check on that, but presumed it wouldn't be permitted. 'Water table is probably too high.'

Two days later, in Home Depot looking for a book on how to build a deck, Jacob saw a book titled Vacation Homes And Cabins. It was a catalog of plans for small houses, most under a thousand square feet. 'Now that's an idea,' Jacob thought. 'A little cabin on the lot. I bet I could build it myself, bit by bit.' He bought the book. He was excited now about something that not long ago, he'd never given a thought.

Jacob mentioned the idea of building a little house to his small group Bible study that week. This was a study made up of three couples and two singles from a couple of local churches.

Jacob no longer led the college ministry Bible study. It seemed better to him to have someone younger lead the study, and Percy was that someone. Jacob had seen Percy gain great skill in guiding a study group to self-discover applicable truth from the Bible. He didn't use Bible studies from the Christian book store, but came up with his own studies through hours of preparation. And Percy had gone one step further, inviting a few key students to join him in preparing the studies.

Jacob thought this idea was brilliant. Young Christians saw a Bible study come together as they discussed a passage of Scripture, with cross references to other key verses. The topic for the study was relevant to the group, and the leader used discussion questions to guide the study. Percy had whimsically declared that the leader should never speak more than 17% of the time. This was a refreshing change from a lot of Bible studies in which the leader did most of the talking.

So Jacob had asked two pastor friends if they'd be okay with Jacob leading what he called a 'leader development' small-group Bible study, using the Gospel of John as the main text. The pastors not only agreed, but both announced the study to their churches. Fifteen people signed up, but it quickly dwindled to eight when they hit Chapter 4 in John. This passage describes Jesus' interaction with the woman at Jacob's well. The application suggested for the group, as an aspect of Christian leadership, was to share the gospel, following Christ's example with the woman at the well. As Jacob had anticipated, several people had found this a bit too challenging. One older lady said, very sincerely, "I don't believe lay people are qualified to preach the gospel like that. That's what pastors do."

Jacob hadn't disputed her comment, but thanked her for it. He was certainly old enough to realize this lady's view on the distinction between laity and clergy was a commonly held belief.

The attenuated group had just discussed John, Chapter 9, concerning the man born blind, to whom Jesus gave sight. Bob and Melinda were an older couple in the group, in their late forties, and Bob was angry about the biblical incident.

"So, let me get this straight; this man has been blind his whole life. It says he's of age, so what's that mean, twenty-five, thirty? So he's blind for twenty-five years, just so God can have a moment of glory?"

Jacob asked, "Does that seem unfair?"

"Unfair? It seems more than unfair. It seems cruel. I don't want to think of God as needing glory so much that He thinks, 'How can I get some glory . . . oh, I know, I'll make this man blind for years!'"

Jacob threw out a question. "Anyone else, on this whole event?"

Jaylen, the single guy, a seminary student said, "Well, yeah, it's a fallen world, and terrible stuff happens, but if you're saying God deliberately made someone blind for the sake of His ego, that wouldn't be the God I believe in. I think it's gotta be something other than that."

Amanda, 26, and a brand new lawyer, said, "When I read Job, I was so confused at how it concluded. I mean, Job never really did get an answer as to why God was doing all that stuff to him. It was just, 'Job, I'm God. You're Job. End of discussion.'"

"Does that seem like the same sort of thing as John 9?" Jacob asked.

"In a way. But the more I thought about it, I was glad the Bible put it like that. I mean, otherwise, we'd feel God owes us answers, and He'd end up explaining Himself to us. I don't think that's how it is. Didn't He say to Job, 'Will you condemn Me so you can be right?'"

Bob looked a little surprised at their comments. "Okay, I'm probably overreacting. I just hate cruelty, and I've seen a lot of it. I don't want to see even a hint that God could be that way."

"I totally agree with that!" Amanda said. "But I don't think He is."

Jacob wondered what cruelty Bob had witnessed that triggered such a strong reaction. If the opportunity came, Jacob would ask. He saw most issues and problems now as a chance to minister to people, not judge them.

"Hey, really good discussion. We'll look at Chapter 10 next week, so read ahead. And read Ezekiel 34 too. The topic is, 'What's a good shepherd do, and how can we be good shepherds?'"

Zeke, husband of the newly married couple said. "The book of the Bible named after me! I'll definitely read that."

Jacob closed in prayer, then said, "Now, for my strange news item. I bought a piece of land out in the boondocks, and I'm thinking of building little house on it. What do you all think? Am I crazy?" Jacob told them the whole story.

Blake thought it was a great idea.

Bob wasn't so sure. "If you build it yourself, it's an endless project. If you hire someone to do it, it's a money pit."

Amanda wondered about building permits and legal issues.

Jacob laughed. "It is sort of a far out idea. I'll definitely let you know what happens."

The next day, Percy texted Jacob. "Got new couple for your Bible study. Gimme call."

Jacob did so. "Who's the new couple, and how'd you know about them? Are they from one of the churches?"

"Nope. This is interesting. They got my number from the website. They're from Indiana, and they said they Googled your name! She's at UCF grad school in nursing. I don't know about him."

"They Googled *my* name? I don't get it. How would they know my name?"

"Not a clue. I guess you're famous even in Indiana."

"Haha! Maybe they're bounty hunters out to get me." Then Jacob said, "If she's at UCF, they could be in the college study if they want. Did you mention that?"

"Oh, yeah. But they said they'd like to be in your small group. Their names are Reuben and Emily Stoltzfus. Think they're Mennonites?"

"Could be. Let me have their cell number, and I'll let 'em know where my house is. Did you tell them we meet in a house?"

"Yup. I hope they're good folks, Jacob."

"Me too."

Jacob met Reuben and Emily at the next Bible study. They were in their early twenties. Emily was blonde, petit, with a gentle smile; Reuben was tall, square-jawed, and serious looking. He had a rough looking beard that needed a lot of filling in. They were dressed very conservatively. Emily had a dress on, and Reuben slacks and blue shirt.

The study that evening was on John, chapter 10, and focused on Jesus as the 'good shepherd.' Both Reuben and Emily contributed to the discussion, and seemed very knowledgeable of Scripture.

Reuben said, "When we talked to Mr. Kowalski, he told us you had assigned John 10, and Ezekiel 34. I think the Ezekiel passage is so clear and powerful. What bad and good shepherds do."

Jacob was impressed. They were prepared for the study, without even having been to the group before. And Jacob was amused by the '*Mr. Kowalski.*'

"Reuben and I discussed this last night," Emily said, "and we decided you can only do three things with sheep: eat them, fleece them, or shepherd them. The bad shepherds did the first two. Jesus was the good shepherd. I don't know about the eating part, but it does seem like some Christians get fleeced."

"That's good!" said Zeke. Then he added, "We're sure glad to have you guys in the study."

"We're glad to be here,"

The study concluded about 9:30, with an assignment to read John 11, the raising of Lazarus, and why Jesus wept even though He knew He was going to bring Lazarus back to life. Reuben and Emily stayed to talk with Jacob.

"Percy told me you'd Googled my name, and that's how you found out about the UCF ministry. By the way, Michael Kowalski goes by 'Percy.'"

Reuben looked puzzled.

"The nickname comes from his liking the poet, Percy Shelley."

Emily said, "But Shelley was an atheist." Then she added, "I like poetry too, but not Shelley!"

Jacob smiled. "Yeah, Percy says he wishes he could go back in time and share the gospel with Shelley.

"So, how did you even know to Google *me*?"

Reuben looked at Emily, as if to say, 'this is your deal; you explain.'

"Jacob, this is complicated. And I feel like I've taken advantage of you, without you knowing."

"How so?"

Emily folded her hands in her lap. "My maiden name is Miller, but my mother's maiden name is Yoder."

"Yoder . . . I knew a Yoder years ago."

"Yes. You knew my grandfather."

Jacob was stunned. "You're Doc Yoder's granddaughter!"

She said seriously, "Yes. Jonathan Yoder was my grandfather. Of course, I never knew him."

"I don't understand. I mean, I'm glad you're both here. But why'd you come to Orlando?"

"How I knew your name is simple. My grandmother had the letter you wrote to her pinned to a corkboard in her bedroom for over two years. Before she remarried."

"She remarried."

"Yes. It would have been unusual in our community not to." Emily continued, "Anyway, my mother remembered your name, and I Googled it. It's an uncommon name, so it wasn't hard to find you."

"You came here to find me?"

Emily didn't answer Jacob's question, but said, "My grandmother was never angry about Grandpa. Years later, when I was in high school, Grandma took your letter out and showed me where you'd crossed out those words. That made her joyful."

Jacob remembered Doc Yoder saying his three-year-old daughter's name. "Your mother is Annie."

"Yes. Annie. Grandma wasn't bitter. But my mother was, and is. When my mother was 15, Grandma had told her that she, Grandma, had prayed hard everyday the whole time he was in Viet Nam, all year. When Grandpa's year was almost up, she felt her prayers had been answered, that he was coming home. Then he signed up for another year, and asked Grandma to pray for *you*. Grandma accepted this as God's will, but my mother didn't. I think Mom almost hated her father because of his decision to stay in Viet Nam . . . and maybe you. She felt, still feels, that her father was taken from her, and somehow links that to you. I know, that's not fair, but it's what it is."

"I still don't understand you guys coming to Orlando."

Emily said, "Reuben and I went to Goshen College. He's a Bible major, and I'm nursing. I want to get my masters in nursing so I can teach, maybe even at Goshen. I love to teach.

"So, I saw online UCF has a really good master's in nursing, and I asked my mother and grandmother if I could come here to study. And meet you and see if my mother could have more of a sense of peace about her father's death—his sacrifice, really."

"Oh, Emily."

"I know." She paused. "My mother doesn't really think a masters is a good idea; she wasn't even crazy about me going to college, but Grandma said I should, and to honor her mother, my Mom agreed.

"That's what I mean by kind of using you as an excuse to come here."

Reuben hadn't said a word. Jacob asked him what he thought about this.

"I don't know. I was surprised Emily's mom agreed to it."

"How long have you guys been married?"

"Six months."

"Oh, my goodness, what a big move to come all the way here."

"It sure is."

Emily looked at her husband with a concerned expression. "This is tough on Reuben. He's been very kind to let me do this."

"What do you want to do, Reuben, long-term?"

"Be a pastor, or a missionary. I know there are two seminaries in Orlando, but I don't know much about them. Or even if I want to go to seminary. I just don't have any clear leading right now."

Jacob said, "Well, this is all totally amazing. Emily, I meant that in the letter to your grandmother. Your grandfather really was the best man I'd ever met."

No one said anything for a moment. Then Jacob said, "I think we should pray that somehow all this will be God-honoring and lead somewhere very clear."

And they did.

*

Jacob had enjoyed leafing through the catalog of small house plans, and had found what he thought was a perfect cabin. It was 20 by 30 feet, a simple rectangle with no complex features. The roof was a steep straight pitch, with enough headroom for a loft, and all the plumbing was on one end of the cabin only. It was utter simplicity. 'I'd definitely put in a fireplace,' Jacob thought. Even though there weren't many really cold days in Florida, Jacob loved the idea of a fireplace.

Reuben had learned of Jacob's scheme to build a little cabin, and seemed eager to help. As it turned out, Reuben was experienced with construction, and even knew how to operate a backhoe, which would be needed for the foundation. He went with Jacob and Percy one day to the lot, and was genuinely excited.

"Man, this is great! It's high enough for you to have a slab foundation. You won't even need a stem wall."

Percy was impressed. "You know how to do this?"

"I grew up with building stuff. And the first vehicle I ever drove was a John Deere tractor. It had a front end loader, and a backhoe." He said to Jacob. "We can rent a backhoe from Home Depot, and do the excavation ourselves. It's fun!"

"Are you serious, Reuben? Can we really do this?"

"Yup. I'd suggest one alteration though. Make the footprint 24 by 32. Just as easy materials-wise, and about 150 more square feet."

Percy said, "Reuben, you da man! I'm not only up for it, I'm down with it!" Then Percy tipped his head back and declaimed in a loud voice, "'My name is Ozymandias. Look at my works, ye mighty, and despair!'"

Jacob said, "I hope we don't . . . despair, that is."

And so began the great building project that Bob had predicted would be endless. But it wasn't. And Jacob was astonished how satisfying the work was. Reuben had a Ford F250 truck, big enough to pull a good-sized trailer, so they were able rent a small backhoe from Home Depot. The employee in charge of rentals quizzed Reuben on his experience with the equipment, and was satisfied that neither the machine nor its operator would come to harm.

The greatest challenge in the early going was getting the building permit. A man in the county office, whom Percy nicknamed 'Cruel Carl' found plenty of reasons not to issue the permit. "If it's a do-it-yourself job, no contractor, you need a lot more details," Carl stated. After the third attempt, Bob from the Bible study put on a coat and tie, and went with Jacob to the permitting office. He just stood next to Jacob, scowling and, as Bob put it, looking lawyer-like. Carl stamped the papers, Jacob paid the fee, and they had the permit!

"We don't need power yet," Reuben said, "but it would be good to go ahead and make the request with Duke for the temp pole and service."

Percy said, "We would be so lost if you weren't here, Reuben!"

Learning to operate the backhoe was enjoyable, especially since excavating for the slab wasn't precision work. Once the stabilizers were down, it was pretty simple to operate the bucket. The cabin would be built in the already cleared quarter acre. Reuben let Jacob and Percy do the grading of the 24 by 32 site, and Reuben did the more careful perimeter trenches for the reinforced edges of the slab.

Reuben commented, " We don't do this kind of foundation up north, but I YouTubed it, and it's quite simple."

When the termite treatment, plastic sheet, and rebar were in place, the building inspector approved, and the slab was poured. Reuben estimated two full ready-mix concrete loads, and he hit it right on the nose.

"If you guys'll level the concrete with the long 2X4, I'll do the bull float work. We'll let it set up a bit, then we get out on it with plywood sheets and do the finishing."

The slab pour took nearly four hours, but it looked good, even to Reuben, who looked at it smiling and said, "Yup! Yup!"

Percy said, "This is awesome. I've never done anything like this."

"The next part is fun too, but more work and slower. The concrete block walls."

The three men only worked weekends and odd days on the cabin. For one thing, the lot was 35 minutes away from UCF. But in six weeks, they had the block walls up, stressed concrete lintels and sills in place, and the roof framed and sheeted. Jacob was surprised and pleased with the renewed energy he had while working on the cabin. Seeing tangible results as they completed different phases of the building was satisfying. And even though Jacob had sore muscles at the end of the day, he thought, as athletes in training would say, 'it hurts good.'

They got the roof inspected and the 'Diamond T Building Wrap' on the roof plywood before the rainy season began. Installing windows and the big sliding doors took only two more weekends.

Jacob, Reuben, and Percy stayed overnight in the 'dried in' cabin on the weekend they'd set aside to do the roof shingles. Percy kept yelling to himself "Sandy side up! Sandy side up!" as they worked the first day. The shingling was made easier because Reuben had rented an air compressor and nail gun. They finished half the roof in the few hours they had on Saturday.

That evening, they grilled burgers and corn for dinner, and slept on the concrete floor with foam pads and sleeping bags.

"Statistically, one of the three of us will snore," Percy said. "I hope it's me."

After two months of working together, the three of them knew each other well. It was a comfortable, open relationship. Reuben had been very impressed with Percy's approach to ministry, and had started going with him on evangelism, and sitting in on the Bible study prep times. "I never knew you could do this kind of thing," he'd commented to Jacob. "This is mind blowing."

Even now, as they stretched out on the floor, they checked each other on Scripture memory. Percy confessed he had an unusual kind of aid to memorizing. "I remember what I hear easily. It's like having a photographic memory, but I'd call it audio-vox instead. If I just read a verse aloud twice, I'll have it."

"That's awesome. What a blessing!" Reuben said.

"Well, maybe. The problem is, I remember too much. I have to turn it off more than I use it. For example, I have millions of brain cells wasted on theme songs from TV shows. Go ahead, name a show . . . "

"Gilligan's Island."

"That's easy. Percy sang with gusto, *Just sit right back and you'll hear a tale, a tale of a fateful trip. It started from this tropic port aboard this tiny ship. The mate was a mighty sailing man, the skipper brave and sure, five passengers set sail that day for a three-hour tour, a three-hour tour. The weather started getting rough, the tiny ship was tossed . . .* "

"Enough! Enough! We believe you."

"The other problem with audio-vox is it doesn't help me to meditate on the meaning of the Scripture. So now I memorize Bible verses the same way you proletariat do."

"Welcome to our world."

Then Percy asked, "Hey, Jacob, if this question is off limits, please tell me, but why didn't you get married?"

Jacob responded quickly. "No, no. That's totally legit. I'm glad you asked. Surprised you haven't before."

Percy hesitated. "Well . . ."

"Are you praying about what to do yourself?"

"Yeah. You're the only single guy in ministry I know, and I wondered why."

"Okay, here goes."

Reuben said, "Don't make this too convincing. Remember, I just got married."

Jacob laughed. "Nope. My basic thinking is that it's good, very good, for people to get married. For one thing, in today's culture, being married is an advantage in ministry. Staying single one's whole life is probably viewed with a bit of suspicion, no wait, that's too strong a word. Let's say at least curiosity."

Percy looked surprised. "Really?"

"Definitely. Not many people have asked me why I didn't marry, but I bet a *lot* have wanted to. But first, more coffee is needed." Jacob suited his words to action.

"I had a Catholic priest friend, who had an Episcopal priest friend. As I'm sure you guys know, Episcopal priests can marry, but this priest didn't. His comment was, 'I never sought it, and God never brought it.' In a way, that's me too, but there's more to it."

Reuben asked, "Why didn't you seek it?"

Jacob said, "I am the way God made me. And . . . "

Percy interrupted. "Wait! Wait! Let me write that down!"

"Haha! Yeah, pretty radical, huh?" Jacob smiled. Then he said seriously, "And a major way that I am is that I *am not* a person who can do two things well. That's why I had to give up my teaching job to do ministry. Same here. I realized I could either do a good job with family, or a good job at ministry, but probably not both. I didn't seek marriage, and God never brought it, because I honestly feel I'd have done a poor job as a family man—husband and father. My focus has been so much on ministry, I just feel being single is best for me."

"The Bible does say married men and women have divided interests," Percy said.

"Yes. First Corinthians 7. And all Scripture is inspired by God, and profitable, so that's still relevant. But I believe for most people, even full-time ministers, marriage is best."

"What's the hardest part of being single? The sex?"

"Sure, but all men have to deal with sexual purity, married or single. Maybe an even bigger issue as the years go by is loneliness. But God has helped me in both. For one thing, like Jesus said, 'Who is my mother and brother? Whoever does the will of My Father who is in heaven, he is my brother and sister and mother.'"

"Where's that verse?" Reuben asked.

"Matthew 12:49, mostly. Anyway, I do have family. It's those who do the will of God, and that's not just some bogus placebo. It's very real. I think of you two men as my family . . . really."

"Thanks, Jacob. That's very helpful. I'd like to get married," Percy said, "but I want to make sure I don't compromise my ministry."

"Michael, I know you pretty well, and I definitely think you're a person who can do more than one thing at a time. Maybe three or four. I wouldn't see you being married as any kind of disadvantage at all."

"Oh, my gosh, Reuben, he called me 'Michael!' That's as official as it gets."

Reuben nodded. "Just lemme know. I'll be your best man. But not this week. I've got a job interview."

"How about next week? Are you free then?"

"What's your wife-to-be's name?"

"Don't know yet."

Jacob laughed. "I'm glad you've given this lots of prayer and thought." And he added, "Reuben, it seems to me that God has led you and Emily together too. That's wonderful."

"Yeah. We've known each other a long time. We're both serious about the Lord, and we did pray for more than a year about marriage."

"Sounds perfect. Good for you guys."

Jacob didn't share a further thought with the two men, but it was one that he'd agonized over. Should Doc Yoder have married? Of course, he couldn't have known he'd die after signing up for another year in Viet Nam, but his dedication to leading men to Christ—to be saved, as Doc had expressed it—was the circumstance that put him at Gun 2 that terrible night. He had left his family alone, forever.

Now Reuben brought up another question. "Can I ask you guys something?"

"Of course," Jacob said.

"The idea for Emily and me coming to Orlando came up pretty fast, and it seemed more like her decision than mine. I mean, I agreed, but it kind of bothers me."

"What bothers you?'

"This probably sounds so bad. But the Bible says the man is to be the leader of his family. I feel like I didn't lead, but got led."

Jacob asked, "Have you talked to Emily about it?"

"No. I guess my question is, am I being, I don't know, too patriarchal about it? I know leadership isn't being the boss, and Emily and I agree on pretty much everything. I just don't feel right about how it happened."

Percy said, "I'm going to offer you some marriage advice. And it's advice untainted by any experience whatsoever . . . talk to Emily."

"But wait for the right time," Jacob added.

"Okay," Reuben said. He paused. "Please pray for me."

Percy was serious now. "We will. We definitely will. It's important."

*

Jacob had introduced the topic of person-to-person discipleship to the small group Bible study after they'd discussed John 15, in which Jesus said He'd appointed His disciples to go and bear fruit.

Over the years, Jacob had codified his discipleship plans to what he called 'the Seven and Three.' It referred to seven disciplines of the Christian life, and three character areas. The character areas were the opposites of the three aspects of sin mentioned in 1 John 2: lust of the flesh, lust of the eyes, and pride. So purity, having God's perspective on money and stuff, and humility, defined godly character.

The seven disciplines were practical things Christians could *do* to walk with God: assurance of salvation, daily times in the Word and prayer, fellowship, structured prayer, Bible study, Scripture memory, and witnessing. Jacob had a concise 'follow-up' plan for each of the disciplines, and Bible studies for the character areas. The plans had a 'message to motivate,' Bible principles, Bible examples, and a practical life application for each of the seven.

Jaylen, the Black seminary student, brought up the question of adaptability, how much the plans could be altered to fit a particular culture, without watering down the biblical concepts.

"I grew up in a really good AME church," Jaylen said, "and I think these plans might come across to some people as heavy on structure, but light on relationship. I mean, they're so specific."

"The UCF leader, Michael, brought up the same point," Jacob said. "He's changed some of the specifics. In his case it's more of a generation thing, rather than adapting to a culture. You might talk with him about what he's done. The plans are tools. If a tool breaks or wears out, or it's not the right tool, get a better one."

"So it's okay to alter these?"

"Sure. To some extent. But pray hard and make sure the focus of the Word isn't weakened. And don't give up too soon on the plans as they are. At least try them as is before you adapt.

"Let me give an example. A few years ago, I got to do a three-month class on discipleship with a big church whose ethnicity and worship practices were different than what I was used to. The pastor told me right off that 'these brothers and sisters are *not* going to do Scripture memory.' So I tried a silly experiment."

"What'd you do?"

"When we discussed assurance of salvation, I read the 1 John 5 passage, that says, *he who has the Son has life . . . I write this to you who believe in the name of the Son of God, that you may know you have eternal life.* Not wonder about or hope, but know." I said, "Why don't you memorize this verse. It's so good.'"

"Did they do it, " Jaylen asked.

"Ah, well. I figured probably not, so at the beginning of the next session, I said, 'We'll be talking tonight about fellowship, but first let me share a distressing thing with you. I was with a guy this week, a young Christian, who was unsure if he was really saved, if he was going to heaven. I knew he'd accepted Christ, but I was totally lost about what to say to him to assure him of his salvation! I didn't know what to tell him!'"

"A lady in the back of the room said, 'But didn't you say last week about if a person had the Son, he had life, and he could know it?'

'Perfect!' I yelled. 'I wish I'd remembered that verse! It would have been so helpful.'"

Jaylen was smiling. "I'm surprised you got away with that."

"Hey, they loved it. So I did that every week. I'd start off with, 'I have a terrible problem! This same guy thinks he doesn't need other believers, that he's fine just by himself. I didn't know what to say to him!!'

"By this time, five or six people had memorized at least parts of verses. 'What about, *woe to the one who falls and there's not another to life him up?*' someone would yell.' It was great."

"I can just picture you doing that. I'm not sure I'm old enough to pull that off, but I'll try some stuff. I'm hearing you say, be creative but don't change it so much the message is weakened."

"Yup. Do whatever's needed to give the Word of God its greatest power."

Reuben did get the job he interviewed for, as Education Coordinator at the church he was attending. "It doesn't pay much, but enough," he told Jacob.

And with the start of a new term at UCF, Percy had much less time available to help Jacob with the cabin. Plus, the fact that the cabin was protected from weather with windows installed and the roof finished, meant Reuben and Percy viewed the project as 'on hold.'

The well and septic system were completed in just two days by contractors, but it was also a significant hit on Jacob's finances. Most of the remaining work would have to be done by him and, when they could, Reuben and Percy. Jacob felt even more of a sense of impatience, and often went out to work on the cabin alone.

Two months went by, and one day, as Jacob was nailing up furring strips on the walls, frustrated that some of the wood strips split as he put them up, he was suddenly overwhelmed by a feeling of futility, a sick awareness of wasted time.

'What am I doing!' he thought. He sat down on a five-gallon paint bucket, and looked around the cabin. The north facing wall was mostly glass, large sliding glass doors, and plate glass windows at the gable above the doors. The framing and the floor of the loft were done. The cabin and wooded site were exactly what he had pictured from the very beginning.

But the awful feeling of wasted days and months persisted. "Oh, Lord, why am I doing this?" Jacob said aloud. He thought, 'I don't have a lot of years left. What am I doing, putting all these hours into a house, and not ministry?' Then another even more terrible thought came to him. Was what he was doing in ministry—indeed, had been doing for forty years—all that fruitful? What had all those years produced? It didn't seem like much. 'What have I accomplished in all those years?'

Jacob thought of Jesus' parable of the four soils, that the first three were unfruitful, but that good soil number four produced thirty, or sixty, or a hundred fold of fruit.

'Thirty fold? Sixty fold! I don't have anything close to that. What am I doing wrong?'

Jacob reflected on the people from past years. Dylan and Kaitlin were retired now, but still doing ministry at Drayton as Life Ministry associate staff.

Seth and Andrea had married, had five kids. Seth was an elder at his local church, and did lead some younger church members out on evangelism at nearby student apartments. He and Andrea had a Bible study with young couples in their home.

Justin had been signed by the Dolphins, then traded to the Cowboys, then to the Eagles, then released. To the best of Jacob's knowledge, Justin was doing no ministry; he was an adjuster with his uncle's insurance agency.

Conner had received his MD at the University of South Florida's medical school, and was a radiologist at the big VA hospital in Tampa. Holly was an adjunct professor of art at The University of Tampa.. Conner had bought two new houses in a modest subdivision, side by side, for Holly and himself. Neither ever married, but they had each other, so that was good. Jacob didn't know if Conner or Holly did any type of ministry, or even if they were in a good local church.

Jacob loved and appreciated each person, but the question 'What have I accomplished?' haunted him. Above all things in life, Jacob wanted to be able to say, at the end of his days, the words Jesus said to the Father in John

17 . . . *I have glorified You on the earth, having accomplished the work You gave me to do.*

Had he done the work God gave him to do? If he was doing ministry wrong, why hadn't God let him know, given new leading? For so many years the ministry goal and vision seemed so clear. Jesus said, 'make disciples'; Paul said 'take the things you got from me and entrust them to faithful men who can teach others as well'; Paul further said, 'ministry means having the loving heart of a mother and the teaching heart of a father.'

It was so simple in the Bible. Make disciples who can make other disciples, and do it with love and truth. This is what Jacob had given himself to do for more than half his life. Now, as he looked at the results, his heart ached. It wasn't like Ephesus, Jacob thought. He hadn't lost his first love. But he was confused, It was so slow. It was so small. It was so puny. It was so . . . inadequate.

"God," Jacob prayed aloud, "How do I hear You? How do I know what You want me to do? If I've wasted the last 40 years, please don't let me waste what's left."

It wasn't a loss of confidence. It was a lack of knowing. Jacob had never felt that he had missed out on anything good in life, something other than ministry, not at all! It was just that now, in his mind, there was a terrible, vague sense of inadequacy. There was that word again! Not inadequacy to *do* ministry, but an inadequacy to know *what to do.*

Doug Cohan had once told Jacob that ministry goals have to be clear. "You can't work hard at something that's not clear. If the vision isn't clear, people dabble at ministry. It's okay to be part-time in ministry, but it's never okay to be half hearted" Doug had said, "Paul had told the church at Corinth, *I'll gladly spend all that I have, and spend myself, for the sake of your souls.* Jacob, that's how we need to be."

Jacob got up off the paint bucket, and knelt before the Lord. "Father, I want clarity for the rest of my life. If I'm doing the right thing, or the wrong thing, please, Father, let me know."

Jacob got up, piled up the rest of the furring strips, locked the door, and left, not knowing when he'd return.

A month later, Jacob got a call from Bob, asking to meet for breakfast. He was the one in the small group who'd struggled with the man born blind in John 9.

"I wanted to tell you why I had such a problem with Jesus and the blind man," Bob said, "way back when in the Bible study."

"Good. Thanks, Bob."

"I've been thinking about this a lot. I remember you saying that in John 11, Jesus wept because He loved Lazarus and his sisters and felt compassion for their suffering about Lazarus dying. But before that He'd told His disciples that He was glad that He'd not been there when Lazarus died, so that His disciples would believe in Him."

"Yes. That's right."

"When He said that, it seemed so heartless, even if it was for a reason." Bob continued. "But even though Jesus knew He'd bring Lazarus back to life, He was still grieved."

"I think so. That's how I see it."

"Jacob, when I was a kid, my mom divorced and remarried. My stepfather was a drunk and a bully. He'd beat up my mom, and there was nothing I could do. I was too small. I remember daydreaming about killing him. He was a sadist. I honestly think the main reason he married my poor foolish mother was to have someone to torment."

"Oh, Bob, I'm so sorry. That must have been awful."

"So that's why it made me really mad to think God made the blind man the way he was, just to get some glory. It just struck me as sick. And I hated that."

Jacob asked, "What do you think now?"

"Well, the John 11 thing was good. I could see a point to Jesus doing what He did, to use a hard thing to help people see He was God. And I was glad to see that it was more than just Jesus being strategic. He was sad about Lazarus dying.

"And," Bob added, "I was impressed with what Amanda said about Job."

"Yeah, that was good. You won't hear many sermons about Job's conclusion: 'I'm God; you're Job. Deal with it!'"

"But, Bob, that's really important," Jacob said. "God is who He is. We can't make Him be who we'd like Him to be. We accept God as the Bible says He is, or we don't believe in God."

"I get it. But why's it that way?"

"Bob, I think one of the biggest issues non-Christians have with God is, if He's so loving, why does He allow terrible things to happen. Like your step-dad's treatment of you mother."

"I *am* a Christian, but that still bothers me. I'd never been in a Bible study like ours, so I don't know a lot, but that's a problem for me."

Jacob opened his Bible to Romans, chapter 1. "Here it says that because people reject God, He 'gave them over to depravity.' To do terrible things. That's harsh, but Bob, what if God *made* people do what's right? What if He didn't allow them to sin?"

"You mean if we had no choice?"

"Yes."

"I guess we wouldn't be made in God's image then."

"Yeah. Like it or not, God has to let humans choose, either to do what's right, wrong, or even terrible stuff."

"Okay."

They were sitting in a restaurant, and Jacob took three of the little coffee creamer cups. "Let's say these are attributes of God. Love, power, and wisdom." He put the little cups in a triangle, and put a saucer on top of them. He took Bob's water glass and put it on the saucer.

"Okay. The water glass is our faith in God. It rests on the three aspects of His nature, or His sovereignty. The Bible says the constant love of God never ceases. It says His wisdom has no limits; that His thoughts are higher than our thoughts. And it says He holds all things together, and nothing is impossible with God. Would you say you see God this way?"

"I guess so. Yes, I do."

"What if you doubted His power? I mean, if you removed the 'power' cup from under the saucer?"

"The water would spill. Our faith." Bob was nodding now. "Same if we had a problem with either of the others."

"Yup," Jacob agreed. "If God's not powerful, He could be loving and wise, but unable to help us when we need it.

"If He's not wise, then He'd be a loving, powerful God, but He wouldn't be smart enough to know what's best for us.

"If he's not loving . . . and maybe this is what you wondered about with the man born blind . . . then we'd have a God who's wise, powerful, but uncaring."

Bob said, with conviction in his voice, "Jacob, I like that. Thanks." He paused. "I'm glad I can believe in a loving God, even if I don't understand why He does things sometimes."

"Yeah. His ways are higher than our ways."

Bob got a text that his high school daughter had forgotten her clarinet for band practice. Could Bob take it to her at school. He thanked Jacob again and left.

"Thank *You*, Lord," Jacob said quietly. "That was good!"

As Jacob drove home, he asked himself which part of God's sovereignty he might struggle with. He was convinced of God's love and wisdom. Did he question the Lord's power, especially His ability to let Jacob know what He wanted Jacob to do? He decided, 'no,' he didn't really doubt that God could easily communicate His will to Jacob. The Scripture was clear and compelling. Maybe it wasn't confusion as much as discouragement. Jacob quoted to himself verses of encouragement. *Do not lose heart in doing good, for in due season we shall reap, if we do not grow weary . . . in the Lord, your labor is not in vain.*

Jacob prayed, "Oh, Father, let me believe these promises, and trust in You."

As autumn came, and the dry season began, Jacob went back to the cabin to work. 'I don't want this to be like the unfinished tower in Luke 14 that people ridicule,' he thought. He was putting up wall board now, a satisfying but tedious job to do alone. He had been staying nights at the cabin, as there was now water, sewer, and electric power.

A pickup truck came down the drive to the cabin. It was Reuben and Emily, Emily driving. "We brought you food, Jacob!" Emily yelled as they got out. "Percy said you were out here."

"What! Thank you! Emily, I've never seen you with glasses. "

"Only for driving. Reuben wants me to get used to this monster." She waved at the F-250, then continued, "Enchilada casserole, plates, forks, and cups."

"Ah, awesome, but I don't have any way to heat it"

"We brought our microwave," Reuben said, as he pulled a huge box from the back seat.

Jacob laughed. "You guys are amazing. You've saved my life. I'm starving."

There were camp chairs and the three of them feasted on Emily's enchilada casserole. "This is *so* good," Jacob said. "It's really nice of you guys."

"Percy said you were working out here alone," Reuben said. He looked around the cabin. "I feel bad that I haven't been more help lately. Hanging sheet rock on the ceiling is hard. I'll help you with that."

"Thanks, but I'm in no rush."

Reuben glanced at Emily and Jacob saw the faintest hint of a nod from Emily. "Percy also said that you were kind of discouraged these days." Reuben said.

Jacob was genuinely touched; they were obviously concerned. 'This is why they came out,' he thought. They were such close friends now, he felt no hesitation in sharing his heart, and struggles, with them.

Jacob said, "He's right. I've been wrestling with some discouragement lately. Well, it's more than *some* discouragement. It's like, at the end of my life, I've evaluated what I've done for the Lord. I'm not very impressed, and that's an understatement."

"How do you mean?" Emily asked.

Jacob took a moment to answer. "Emily, when I started in ministry, I was so confident that I was doing exactly what God had called me to. Honestly, I was so sure about it that I was pretty dismissive of other people's ministries. Yeah, I know, that's so arrogant, but I didn't see it that way. I thought what God has asked me to do was *so* important, I didn't take much interest in what God had apparently asked others to do."

"I'm not sure that's arrogant, Jacob," Reuben said. "Your vision for ministry *is* really good. Emily and I are grateful we came down here, and get to be part of what you and Percy are doing."

"Well, good. I'm glad to hear that." Jacob said. "But it's so small. I've questioned lately if this really is part of God's plan, why doesn't He help it grow? During the early years, I saw what I was doing as laying a foundation, and that big things would happen eventually. But it's been forty plus years, and it still seems like all I'm doing is laying a foundation. I hate to say this, but it's made me doubt if I'm doing what God wants."

Reuben put this plate down and moved his chair closer to Emily. "Emily and I have been talking about this."

Emily smiled. "In fact, we've been talking about nothing else for a week."

"First of all," Reuben said, "my job at the church has been good. I appreciate what they're doing. I asked the pastor what his goal for the church was."

"What 'd he say?"

"He said, 'I have two goals. One, from 2 Peter, to help people escape the corruption that's in the world. And second, to build community.'"

"That's good," Jacob said. "I'm impressed he's got it so clear."

"It is. But I definitely think what *you're* doing is also essential. Different, but essential. You'll probably never have as big a group as the church, but your goal is different."

Reuben turned to Emily. "Tell Jacob your thought about the local church and Life Ministry."

Emily spoke up. "I like the idea of community. It's for everyone, from babies to old people. But what struck me was the pastor's comment about helping people escape. That's what Moses did. He was God's man to get the people out of the slavery of Egypt."

"Yeah, I sure agree with that."

"So Moses was the leader of large group of people. Not many of them did very well, but God's role for Moses was to lead them.

"Jacob, what if God's role for you is not to be a Moses, but an Abraham? He was God's man too."

Jacob was taken by surprise. Had he been so prideful to have not seen this? He'd never even thought of it. "You mean . . . ?"

"I think you're Abraham, not Moses."

Reuben said, "Keep going, Emily."

"Both did what God wanted them to do, but Abraham didn't lead a huge group; he was the start of many generations. So it doesn't matter how small or difficult the beginning is. Abraham sure didn't have an easy job of it. He was old, and God even asked him to sacrifice his ministry, so to speak."

Jacob had a sudden deep conviction that what they were sharing with him was right, profoundly right. There was a sense of God speaking to him through the insight of these two young Christians. He felt grateful to God, and them, for what they were saying.

"Emily. Reuben. You don't know how much this helps."

God's Word, and the testimony of godly people had confirmed Jacob's call and heart for ministry.

"We're glad," Reuben said. And he added, "I was thinking of John, the baptizer, too. What a pathetic ministry he had, in terms of impressiveness. He ate honey and bugs, had a lousy wardrobe, announced Jesus, and was beheaded at the whim of a dancing girl. No offense, Jacob, but what you do for the Lord isn't about you. John said, 'He must increase. I must decrease.' But Jesus called John the greatest man ever born of woman. I think it was because he did exactly what God's role for him was."

No one spoke for a while. Then Jacob said quietly, "I've always believed the Bible was clear about this ministry. I've never considered it being like Abraham. Thank you. I'm very grateful for what you've said."

Emily put her hand on Reuben's arm. "Now, let me tell you something about Reuben and me.

"Jacob, I told you a year ago that we came here so I could meet you and help my mother to have more peace. That's true. I wanted to tell my mother, 'It was worth it, what Grandpa did.' But there was something more too. I know I was thoughtless of Reuben's leadership. We came here because of me. Because of what I felt.

"I had a fear. I was fearful that Reuben would be like my grandfather, that he would be so dedicated to ministry that he'd somehow, someway, do what Grandpa did. And I'd be left alone. I didn't even want us to have children. I was so afraid."

Reuben smiled. "But that changed. Didn't it, Em?"

"Yes. It changed."

"What happened?"

Reuben said, "Well, you know I've been showing Em the 7 and 3 discipleship plans, and we've gone to student apartments a lot. Emily loves going to talk with students!"

"I do."

"Here's something you don't know. We took Zeke and Erika out on evangelism last night, and they were blown away. Zeke was amazed. They want Emily and me to disciple them."

"Oh, man! That's wonderful!"

Emily said, "Jacob, I think what my grandfather did *was* worth it. He was an Abraham too. Even if God has it be the same for Reuben and me . . . it's worth it."

Reuben said quickly, "So here's our plan, with your approval. Emily gets her degree in ten months, and she's already been offered a nursing job at Shands hospital in Gainesville."

"Ah," Jacob said, "I wish you could stay in Orlando."

"What we'd like to do," Reuben continued, " is to get ministry training from Percy for this coming year, then start a ministry at the University of Florida in Gainesville, just like this one."

"What! Really?"

"Yup. Are you okay with that?"

Jacob' heart rejoiced. "That's the best thing I've heard in a long time. That would be truly good. Thank you. Thank you both."

Reuben smiled and said, "I know Percy is your Isaac. But maybe I could be your Jacob, Jacob."

*

Jacob and Percy sat again on the grass in front of the UCF library. Percy was telling Jacob, seriously this time, about Calli, the beautiful, godly girl with whom he was smitten.

"She knows all about our ministry, Jacob, and she's totally excited about it. She's wonderful."

"I believe it."

They had discussed the plan for Reuben's and Emily's training. Percy had accepted a teaching position in English at Smithsbury College, a Christian university that was opening a campus in Orlando. This meant he could continue the UCF ministry, including evangelism, without worrying about any perceived conflict of interest. "I can even recruit young Christians at Smithsbury to Life Ministry. It fits in perfectly with training Reuben and Emily."

Jacob said, "That is so good, Percy!" Then he added, "One more thing. I prayed about the cabin, and decided to deed it over to Reuben's church. The pastor was so excited. He said it was an answer to prayer. But he said we can use it anytime for ministry retreats and stuff."

"Hey, that is so awesome! Good for you, Jacob."

Jacob had asked Percy if he was willing to assume the overall leadership of Life Ministry, to include traveling to Gainesville to help Reuben and Emily, and to go down to encourage Dyland and Kaitlin on a regular basis.

Percy had said, "That would be a privilege. Thanks for trusting me with that, Jacob."

Well, I ain't gonna live forever. It's time to pass it on."

Percy asked Jacob a question. "Jacob, do you think about dying? You're not that old, and you're healthy."

"In a way, I do. Obviously, I'm not afraid of dying. Like Paul said, being with the Lord face to face is very much better.

"But, Percy, I'll tell you one thing I am afraid of. In fact, I dread it."

Percy looked surprised. "What's that?"

"Senility. Percy, I hate the idea of losing my mind. My mother had Alzheimer's in her last years and it was terrible. Every week, I'd find six dessert plates with apple pie set out on the table, like for a party. She'd always say, 'I didn't do that!' And she thought there was woman living in her closet because she'd see her reflection in the mirror on the closet door."

"That's sad."

"So that's what I'm fearful of."

"I bet it won't happen to you," Percy said.

"I hope not. I would truly hate that."

Percy said, "Let's pray right now. " And Percy did pray, that Jacob would not become senile. The two brothers in Christ prayed for God to be glorified through their lives.

*

God did give Jacob more years of life, fruitful years of ministry. And Jacob felt in his heart he would be able to say to the Father, *I have accomplished the work You gave me to do.*

The thing Jacob dreaded—the diminishing of his ability to think clearly— did happen. But it wasn't as bad as he'd feared, because he died soon after his mind began to fail.

At the end, a nervous young chaplain entered his room in the VA hospital. In a last lucid, intuitive moment, Jacob became aware of the chaplain, and thought, 'Oh, It's his first death! And he doesn't know if I'm saved.' So Jacob cried out, "When I came to Christ, they called me 'El T!"

The chaplain relaxed, smiled, and. put his hand on Jacob's shoulder. He said, "God bless you, El T."

And a little while later, Jacob went to be with the Lord.

Epilogue

Sister Angelique left Viet Nam and returned to France in October of 1974, as the outcome of the war became evident. She was overjoyed to be received into a convent school near her two younger brothers, her only remaining family. She died in Troyes in 1995, of a brain aneurysm. During her years in Nha Trang, she had prayed for many soldiers, one of whom was Jacob Saith.